Key to the Lighthouse Cornerstone

The Sea Crest Lighthouse Series

Book Three

Carolyn Court

Kindle Create Publishing

Carolyn Court

Enjoy!

The Key to the Lighthouse Cornerstone

Book 3 of The Sea Crest Lighthouse Series.

ISBN:13   979-8353607243

ASIN: BOBFVKLB3L

Cover design by: Mylène Charpentier

The Sea Crest Lighthouse Series:

The Heart of the Lightkeeper's Daughter Book One

The Lightkeeper's Secret Book Two

The Key to the Lighthouse Cornerstone Book Three

Dedicated to a remarkable friend,

Jeanette Embrey

Jeanette, thanks for always supporting my writing.

Thanks for your encouragement to write Grace and Joe's story for

The Key to the Lighthouse Cornerstone.

You're always in a great mood with a fantastic sense of humor.

I am always thankful for your generosity.

I'm blessed to call her my friend!

Chapter 1

A chilling flood of distress washed over her as the sharp edge slashed her finger. Grace felt pure agony as she watched the offending bottle slip from her hand. She pleaded, "Please don't break as she watched it fall toward the jagged rocks below.

She jerked her bloody, cut finger to her mouth and leaned out over the railing, crying, "Oh, no! What have I done?"

"No! No! No!" she screamed as her legs raced down the broken walkway from the Sea Crest Lighthouse to the rocky shoreline, but her eyes never left the antique glass. *"It's only 15 feet away. I've got to catch it,"* she thought as she flung out her arms and shouted, "Wait!"

She watched the falling container as it smashed to smithereens!

Grace slowed her pace as she dejectedly stomped her feet in the sand and wondered, *"Why couldn't I get to you in time?"* She looked ahead to the scrunched-up disaster in time to spot a delicately wrapped roll of paper tumbling from the crushed glass fragments. At last, free of the wreckage, the pale parchment was caught by a gust of wind and danced along the sand beneath the Sea Crest Lighthouse.

"This message is over one hundred years old! I can't lose it," she cried as she flew down the beach and raced after it.

Finally, she caught up with the sandy, crumpled paper. She bent to touch it, cautiously raised it, and softly whispered, "Now, let's see what was so important that they put you into the cornerstone of our Sea Crest Lighthouse."

Grace carefully unwrapped the old twine from the rolled-up parchment. The binding practically fell apart in her hands. However, it revealed a wax seal, which was still set as firmly as the day it was stamped. Her eyes fell on the beautiful interwoven letters, RLS. Grace's hands trembled as she recognized this as the most famous Scottish Lighthouse family of the mid-1800s.

"Wow!" Grace could hardly believe their good fortune as she whispered, *"RLS – Robert Louis Stevenson."*

She was elated as she unrolled the precious letter. She began to read, *"My father, Thomas Stevenson, drew up the plans to build the Tahiti Lighthouse on the site of Captain James Cook's observation conservatory. Our Stevenson family has retained close ties with Captain James Cook's Scottish family.*

Grace was shocked. Her father was named James Cook, and it was whispered that she was also a descendant of her father's ancestry line. Once in a while, they questioned whether it was true or not. Still, it had always been terrific to pretend with each other and anyone else who would believe them. She had once tried to connect their bloodlines, but the time constraints were too much at the time. Grace hadn't gotten back to the project yet.

Grace remembered, *"In fact, my father had wanted to travel to Tahiti to view the 2014 phenomenon of the transit of Venus across the Sun. This was visible from Tahiti and rarely occurred. This trip would have been a once-in-a-lifetime opportunity for my father. Sadly, he could not actually make that*

*trip. Still, we continued researching Captain James Cook's
voyages and The Islands of French Polynesia."*

Her previous research had uncovered that in Captain James
Cook's ancestry line, many ancestors, including his own mother,
were named Grace.

She picked up the cherished letter again and continued
reading. *"My grandfather placed a unique locket inside the
hollowed-out cornerstone of The Pointe Venus Lighthouse. It's
located on the northern tip of Tahiti in the Society Islands, French
Polynesia. It was built in 1868. It is the key to a valuable keepsake
locket, which holds a picture of Captain James Cook. The key will
be passed down through future generations by the ancestors of the
James Cook Family.*

*In the future, when the cornerstone is recovered, and the
locket is found, it can only be opened with the key that his
ancestors possess. The locket has a picture of his mother, Grace
Cook, and his father, James Cook, in a separate, hidden locket
compartment. This secret opening can only be unlocked with the
bit or end piece of the skeleton key. It will slide up and release an
additional tiny key that has been filed and cut. This unique design
will fit, slip into the edge, and open the inside with his parent's
pictures. This will verify the lineage chain for their family when the
cornerstone's locket is opened with the ancestor's key*

Grace was stunned as she vaguely wondered about an old
Victorian key from her paternal grandmother. *"I haven't even
thought about that key in ages. It's funny, but we never did
discover what that key opened."*

*"Well, it's just too wild to even think about. I'm sure my
grandma's key is Not this mysterious ancestral connection to
Captain James Cook's family. After all, it's been among several
pieces of costume jewelry of no significant value that was kept
inside her jewelry box. My dad's family certainly wasn't wealthy
by any means. We eventually agreed that Grandma found the
beautiful 'orphan' trinket with the pretty blue stones was too pretty
to part with, even if it didn't fit anything.*

"However, the peculiar feeling lingered as she held the precious letter. She turned and regarded the Sea Crest Lighthouse with solemn deliberation. *"I'm a historian. I work with documented facts. I operate within the framework of available information and form opinions based on highly educated reasoning."*

She shifted her focus to the cresting waves of the ocean as if they held the answer to her dilemma. Still, her eyes soon returned to the magnificent tower. Grace gathered strength in her decision and thankfully concluded, *"I can't help myself. I have to trust my instincts on this one. My gut feeling has never been stronger."*

Her proclamation inspired her to promptly pull out her phone and scroll thru the telephone numbers. "This might be the most important step of my life," she affirmed with joy as she dialed.

"Hello," she said excitedly when the reservationist answered. "I need to book a seat on your next flight to Tahiti."

"Well, let me check," said the reservationist. "The only flight that will connect to this afternoon's Air Tahiti Nui, flight in Los Angeles, is leaving here in two hours. It will arrive in Papeete, Tahiti, at 9:45 PM."

"Wow! I'll have to hurry, but I'm sure I can make it. Book a seat on that flight, plus the connection to Tahiti. I'll return in one week."

They completed the travel arrangements, including transportation to the Hilton Hotel Tahiti, where Grace planned to stay for the first two nights. After that, she'll find a convenient place to stay near the Tahiti Lighthouse.

Grace looked at her watch as she practically ran back to the lighthouse. "I need to pick up my passport and pack a couple of things, but I'd better let Michael know what I found in the cornerstone before I leave."

Michael was the new husband of one of her best friends, Kate. He was a world-famous architect for his career working on lighthouses and other structures. His company was repairing the Sea Crest Lighthouse, damaged in a storm. Late yesterday the workers discovered the cornerstone in the damaged ruins.

Kate and Michael were sharing a thermos of coffee when Grace breathlessly hurried up to them. "Boy, you won't believe what I found in the dark glass bottle from the cornerstone."

"What have you got there," asked Kate as she looked down at her hands.

"You'll never guess," announced Grace with great excitement. "Wait, on second thought, I don't have time for a guessing game," she continued as she carefully handed the ancient wax seal to them. "Do you know what that is?" she whispered proudly. Without skipping a beat, she charged on, "okay, I'll tell you."

"Hey. Slow down a minute and let me look," Kate laughed.

"Yeah, what's the big hurry?" laughed Michael. "That cornerstone has been buried for over one hundred years."

Grace drew her hand to her pounding heart as she whispered, "Well, this is Robert Louis Stevenson's seal. He directed that this letter be placed in our cornerstone of the Sea Crest Lighthouse."

Kate was shocked. "What? 'THE' Robert Louis Stevenson? Our lighthouse?"

Mary Beth, another close friend of the two women, arrived in time to hear the last comment. "Hey, what's all the fuss about?" she asked.

"Grace found this rolled parchment letter with the RLS wax seal. She claims it stands for Robert Louis Stevenson."

"Nice. I was hoping I'd get here in time to see what you found in the cornerstone," exclaimed Mary Beth. "What an amazing discovery!"

"Okay," Grace practically shouted. "You catch each other up with the Robert Louis Stevenson find. He also placed something related to this in the cornerstone of The Venus Pointe Lighthouse in Tahiti. It was constructed in 1867 and underwent extensive renovations a hundred years later, in 1965. I plan to determine if the cornerstone was located during the repairs and what was done with the contents. I have a reservation for a flight that leaves in a couple of hours. I also need to make a copy of this letter to take to Tahiti."

"Well, we turned off the electric power to make repairs," started Michael.

"That's okay," said Mary Beth. "I can help, even though I don't understand your sudden trip to Tahiti. I'll stop by my real estate office and make a copy for you. Then, I can swing by your house and give you a ride to the airport if you'd like."

"Thanks, I'll take you up on that. I'll explain everything to you when you pick me up," replied Grace.

Chapter 2

Fifteen minutes later, Grace enthusiastically packed like a mad woman in her bedroom. She dialed her friend Maggie and promptly put her on speaker as she breathlessly exclaimed, "You'll never guess what was hidden in an old bottle, in the cornerstone!"

Grace said, "We did get the cornerstone open and found a hand-written note from Robert Louis Stevenson. It explains that his father, Thomas Stevenson, had repaired the Tahiti Lighthouse around the same time Sir Michael Chambers and Joe Walsh had built our Sea Crest Lighthouse. The Stevenson Lighthouse Dynasty was very close friends with Joe Walsh, the Irish Architect who had sailed to America with blueprints of several different lighthouses.

"My next piece of exciting news is that I'm at my house packing. Just try to guess where I'm going!"

"I know you weren't planning to go anywhere as of last night, so it must be a new development," Maggie laughed.

"I'm going to Tahiti to see if the cornerstone was found when they repaired the Tahiti Lighthouse in 1965. If so, did they discover the locket that Robert Louis Stevenson is writing about?"

"You mean you're leaving right now?"

"Yes! I need to know if they even know about its secret compartment in their cornerstone. If so, what happened to the locket that was inside."

7

Maggie asked, "Do you think it was put in a museum? Yes, you're right. There are all kinds of unanswered questions. Does the original lighthouse site have the same footprint as the current one? Was the new construction added to the lighthouse? Some newer lighthouses are built on a completely different site due to changes in the land or the water."

Grace stated proudly, "The Venus Point Lighthouse is dedicated to Captain James Cook. You'll never believe the strange connection my family may have to this situation. We may have the key to a locket that holds his picture and family crest. The note says, *This key unlocks Captain James Cook's family's locket, which shall be passed down to his ancestors. In the future, we'll honor his family, and they shall join the key with the locket, and that descendant shall be the keeper of the locket for the Cook Family.*

"The Venus Point Lighthouse in Tahiti was built in 1868. Due to extensive damage over time, it had to be restored and extended in 1963."

The doorbell rang, and Grace declared with joy, "Well, I've got to run. Mary Beth is here to take me to the airport. I'll call you later!"

After a mad dash to the car, they looked at each other and broke out laughing. "Oh wait," yelled Grace as she leaped back out of the vehicle. "I forgot my survival kit!"

The Mah Jongg friends, Maggie, Grace, Mary Beth, and Kate, had made 'Survival Kits' for a joke. However, Maggie had been a real-life saver when she shared her own adventure of a life time with James. Her survival skills were crucial in surviving their days when they were trapped together in a section of the Underground Railroad. They discovered the caves and tunnels hidden for over one hundred years.

Grace made her retrieval and returned to the car in record time. "I added some extra things and put my kit in my little backpack."

"What a great idea. That's perfect."

8

"Thanks. I didn't think I'd use it so soon, but it's ready!" Grace laughed.

Mary Beth dreamily disclosed, "Well, I am extremely jealous. I always wanted to revisit Paris in the springtime. The trip that my sister, Monique, and I took to France was life-changing in many ways."

Grace chimed in, "Yes, I remember when you took that trip. I knew you had studied French with me. In fact, we were in French Club together for a couple of years. You often mentioned that you'd love to go to France. I was so excited that you got the opportunity, but don't think I wasn't good and jealous over it at the time too."

"Oh yes," continued Grace. "Now I remember. Didn't your folks give you and Monique the trip as a reward for your hard-earned grades?"

"Yes," Mary Beth laughed as she explained. "While we were visiting the French countryside with all its delightful architecture, I discovered my love of houses and decided to go into the real estate business. I also developed my taste for French Country design, which has never left me. I especially treasure decorative kitchens. The covered stove hoods with their elegant carved motifs are outstanding. I savored the cozy kitchens with the warm fireplaces and enjoyed the expansive kitchen islands, ideal for family gatherings."

"We stayed at bed and breakfasts and took advantage of sharing the evening meals with the innkeepers. We could explore the historic cities and towns daily while returning to observe a glimpse of French life each evening. We felt welcome and safe and knew we were enjoying the trip of a lifetime. Of course, I discovered that this tiny sample was not enough. I have always longed to return.

One of our favorite afternoons was spent with Maria, the delightful hostess of the bed and breakfast where we were staying. She had the long loaves of French bread delivered twice a day. This was the custom in the countryside. The bread was left in a long tubuluer, roadside boxes that resemble rural mailboxes. This was to ensure the freshness factor, essential to all French cooking.

"One afternoon, we were invited to go to town with her. Of course, Monique and I jumped at the opportunity to see where the locals shopped," Mary Beth laughed. "We were not disappointed either!"

"Our first stop was The Pasteries Bakery. As we stepped past the door, our senses were alive at the sight of the vast spread of sweet treats in which to indulge, blended with the aroma of fresh baked goods filling the air. The displays of croissants, eclairs, canele (canelé), and mille-feuille with strawberries and mascarpone were just the start.

"Maria turned and pointed out the displayed sticker on the window, "Artisan Boulanger." This signifies that the Boulanger (a bread maker in France) is the real deal and that the bread will be made on the premises.

"My sister and I watched as they pulled a tray of large puffy braided brioche from the ovens. They had sizeable round rye loaves cooling on the shelves and sourdough bread and baguettes. Bon appétit!

"Well, we finished shopping and walked down to a corner store for a few additional items. This was not a fancy place, but we saw quite a few locals as we made our way down the aisles. We passed a large display of bread that looked identical to the loaves delivered that morning to our bed and breakfast.

Mary Beth chuckled as she continued, "Maria slowly came to a stop as she carefully inspected the exhibit."

"Monique and I watched in awe as she roughly grabbed an offending loaf and pounded it on the table as she yelled, "This is No Good! No Good!" With the final pulverizing blow, the loaf broke in half. She showed us the proof as she exclaimed matter-of-factly, "See? No good!"

"Monique and I glumly looked at the bread and blindly agreed. It was somehow not good enough. We nodded our heads slightly and muttered something that our comrade took for our acknowledging the despicable transgression we had just encountered. Our sweet host nodded her approval at us as she promptly threw it back on the heap in disgust.

"Her eyes flashed indignantly as she marched through the store, with us in tow. Strangely, no one else in the store even batted an eye. It seemed as if this was normal behavior for the French when they came across any bread that was a couple of hours old.

The next shopping experience that day proved that the French would take no prisoners when it came to the quality of their food. We ventured into the shop, which had a fantastic display of chocolates. My sister and I planned to buy a few pieces. As it turned out, our host wasn't satisfied with the quality and promised to make us chocolate mousse that evening.

"Long story short, she did make us the absolute best dessert of my life. We are genuine chocoholics, and that was the crème de la crème!

"We still laugh about our introduction to the authentic French mindset regarding food.

"I think it would be romantic to stroll along the Champs-Elysees with my beau. It's arguably, the most famous avenue in the world. I secretly hope to get engaged to the man of my dreams as we overlook the Seine River from one of its many bridges. I genuinely think the best one is Pont Alexandre III. "

Mary Beth silently lapsed into memories of her favorite guidebook. She remembered the exact words, *"In French, 'pont' means bridge. The Pont Alexandre III is a deck arch bridge that spans the Seine in Paris. It connects the Champs-Élysées quarter with those of the Invalides and Eiffel Tower. The bridge is widely regarded as the most ornate, extravagant bridge in the city. It has been classified as a French Monument Historique since 1975. "*

"Well, Mary Beth, it's certainly no secret," interrupted Grace. "Paris is always at the top of your wish list of trips to take."

"Well, I think it's very unfair. First, Maggie traveled to Europe as an FBI Special Agent to help French couture designers with numerous designs stolen by counterfeiters. Now you high-tail it off to investigate a century-old mystery involving a lighthouse in French Polynesia.

Chapter 3

She changes planes in LAX and again has a tight connection, but she leaves a message for Joe, "Hi Joe. It's Grace. I wanted to touch base with you about my spur-of-the-moment trip to Tahiti. I'll probably be gone for a week. I'm so excited about the note from Robert Louis Stevenson that I found in the cornerstone this morning. I don't know if anyone explained the possible connection between Captain James Cook and Robert Louis Stevenson. I need to investigate the Venus Point Lighthouse in Tahiti. They may have discovered his Cook Family locket when the lighthouse was repaired in 1969. My family may be in possession of the key to it. We may be related to Captain James Cook!"

Next, she called Maggie, "Hi, Maggie. I have a layover in Los Angeles, and I need to speak to James if he's around. Did you tell him about my impromptu trip to Tahiti?" She laughed.

"Yes! and he's so excited about what you found in the cornerstone of the Sea Crest Lighthouse today. We hope your investigation goes well."

"Thanks. I planned a few things while I was on the first leg of this flight. We're about ready to take off from Los Angelos to Tahiti, but could you put him on the line for a minute?"

Maggie handed the phone over to James.

"Wow, Grace! I can't believe you found that note from Robert Louis Stevenson! Who knew he was acquainted with The Chambers' Family?"

"I know, I wasn't expecting it either, but the dates all lineup, and they are both from Scotland. The whole Stevenson Family was involved in building lighthouses. It would make sense that they knew each other."

"Great! How can I help?"

"I remembered a conversation I had with your friend, Jeffery Williams. You know, your attorney from New York City? When he was at Sea Crest for Kate's wedding celebration, he offered to help me with any historical or ancestry research I might need."

"You know, Grace, you're right, now that you mention it. He spends his leisure time teaching and researching."

"Well, James, I don't have his contact information, but I'd like to be able to have his help on this if he has the available time. He might have more access to information from his experience or available resources than I have access to from Tahiti. Could you try to get ahold of him for me? If he agrees, I'll tell you how he can help me."

"Oh, Grace, I'm sure he'll have time for you. He was very impressed with your knowledge about the Parachute wedding gowns and Kate's wedding dress."

"Great! I also left a message for Joe that I was on my way to Tahiti. He was going to come over to the Sea Crest Lighthouse after work to see if we were able to get into the cornerstone. Could you try to reach him for me?"

"Sure, it will be my pleasure." James was already thinking, *"Oh, Yes! What fun we're going to have. Maggie and I would love to 'pay back' our dear friends for all the times they set us up at Kate and Michael's wedding celebration.*

"Great," replied Grace. "I'm going to have my phone off during this flight, which gets in very late tonight. I'll need to catch up on a little sleep for my jetlag. Could you ask if he can call me tomorrow at The Tahiti Hilton Resort at about 4pm Tahiti time? Hopefully, I'll have some information about my schedule and get the answers about the cornerstone by then."

"Sure, I'll make sure he gets the message."

Grace leaned back in her seat to peacefully rest; however, she did not relax enough to feel settled. Granted, she was still very excited about Tahiti, but she felt something was missing. She blinked her eyes open as a quiet thought came to her. *"I wish Joe was here."*

Grace contemplated this realization. *"Well, that's strange. I guess it's unfamiliar to do something this big without him. We usually do things together, and that feels right."*

"When did I start to care enough to miss him?"

Just then, the flight attendant stopped beside Grace. She bent and said softly, "Hello, Grace Cook? You paid for a costly, last-minute ticket. The Business Class Cabin is almost empty, so if you'll, please accompany me, we'll reseat you."

"Thank you," said Grace as she followed the lady to get resettled.

Chapter 4

That afternoon Attorney Joe Lawrence walked down the steps from the courthouse and casually glanced at his phone. He was alarmed at all the messages. He had to have his mobile phone off all day while in court.

Now he quickly scrolled down to Grace's message from this morning. Joe read the news that Grace is on her way to Tahiti. Then he got James' message that Grace wanted him to call her at The Hilton Tahiti Resort tomorrow afternoon at 4 PM.

He'd been out of touch with Grace all day, but he was surprised to be experiencing a feeling of loss. *"How strange,"* he thought sadly. *"Was Grace turning into his best friend?"*

"I'm happy that she has this exciting trip to Tahiti to research the Robert Louis Stevenson cornerstone locket and try to find the answers, but why do I miss her so much?"

"I concede that Grace and I make a terrific dynamic duo!" Joe smiled, *"I love the feeling I get when our plan comes together. I guess a part of me feels left out of this wonderful trip. I can't believe how much I want to be with her for this adventure."*

This feeling of loss did not leave him all evening. In fact, Joe Lawrence would continue to ponder this revelation as he tossed and turned all night!

Chapter 5

The following day, Grace called her mom and dad. "Hey, Dad. You'll never guess where I am!"

Her dad laughed as he answered, "Well, I'll guess you're at the Sea Crest Lighthouse trying to get into that cornerstone. That's all I've heard about for the past week. What did you find?"

"Oh, Dad, I'm not going to tell you what I found, but you aren't even close on your answer of where I am."

"All right, I get another chance. I still think you're somewhere near the lighthouse. Wait, you're at the Sea Crest Restaurant."

"No! But that's a good guess. I'm somewhere you planned to come to a couple of years ago. It was a big deal, and you had to cancel your trip at the last minute."

"What on earth are you talking about, Grace? The only trip I had planned a couple of years ago was to the Tahiti Lighthouse. It's where Captain James Cook set up his observatory to watch the Transit of Venus during his second trip to Tahiti. The observatory was converted into a lighthouse, which still exists today."

"That's it, Dad! I'm in Tahiti! It's absolutely breathtaking! Please, why don't you and Mom come too?"

"What are you talking about? Are you really in Tahiti?"

Yes, put Mom on the phone!"

"Hello, Dear," her Mom exclaimed with excitement. "What is going on? Are you really in Tahiti? Your dad took off to find our suitcases!"

"Well, Mom, I want you to both come to Tahiti. I'm checking on a connection between what I found in the cornerstone of our Sea Crest Lighthouse and the lighthouse here in Tahiti. The one here was repaired in the 1960s, and something related to our lighthouse was put in this cornerstone."

"Well, your dad is eager to join you, and of course, I'm thrilled."

"Great!.... Now, if Dad can't hear you, I'd like you to do a favor for me."

"Of course; what do you need?"

"Mom, I'm not sure if it will mean anything, but I need you to find something and bring it to me when you come."

"Sure, what do you want?"

"Well, Mom, I'm not sure, but I think it may be in your safe deposit box at the bank."

"All right, Grace! What's going on? Do you need money? Has someone kidnapped you?"

"No! No! That's not it. But please don't get Dad involved. I don't want to spoil the surprise."

"What surprise?"

"Sh…, Mom, I don't want Dad to hear us. Do you remember when Grandma left a box of miscellaneous costume jewelry for Dad in her will?"

"Oh, let me think. Do you mean that shoebox that had an assortment of nice things?"

"Yeah, that's it. It had lots of things, but mostly neat things Grandma had saved. Like an old-fashioned compact that was completely empty and a tube of Orange Blossom lipstick by Avon. It was a pastel coral shade that was marvelous. I even remember a special clear blue marble. It was about the size of a quarter. Everything in that box was unique and special."

"I know what you mean," replied her mother. "Your dad's family wasn't well-to-do, but his mom always looked very attractive and well put together. I can't believe she had anything of great monetary value to anyone outside of our family. They weren't rich by any means. I'm pretty sure the jewelry that looked expensive was not real."

"You're probably right; however, could you check around and see if you can locate a jewelry case with an old key with those blue stones? I can't remember all the things in the shoebox. Still, I vaguely picture an elaborate key that doesn't fit any lock Grandma had."

"Yes, I know what you're talking about. I think it's in our safe deposit box at the bank. I can get it for you when we go to retrieve our passports."

"They might have an important piece of history that is valuable to our family. Now, I'd like you both to grab your passports and get on the next flight out."

"I might have a special surprise for Dad. Remember, don't say a word!

Chapter 6

A gentle fresh breeze swept over Grace as she stepped into the lush outdoor lobby. It resembled a tropical oasis with a winding flagstone walkway. Her face felt a fresh mist from a waterfall as she passed by.

She stepped out of the sweeping vista and gazed down where the sandy shore was swallowed up by the gentle waves. She meandered down the winding flagstone walkway as she breathed in the pleasant scent of Tahiti tiare (often referred to as Tahitian gardenia). Her eyes gazed at the fabulous flora and fauna floral design as she reached out to touch a delicate blossom.

"Wow! It's a pleasure to see the colorful mix of hibiscus, frangipani, heliconia, orchid, ginger, and jasmine. These Tahiti flowers are everywhere! My, the beauty takes my breath away," she thought. *"It looks just like a postcard."*

She surveyed the beautiful scenery and spotted a young man down by the dock working on his seaplane. Since she has a small plane pilot's license, she is interested in this little yellow plane.

Nothing was revealed behind the dark lens of his sunglasses as the man looked her way. He wiped a smudge off the bright yellow propeller. He appeared to not have a care in the world as he hummed a pleasant song but said nothing to her while he observed her approach the dock. *"She looks American. Surely she's traveling with a companion."*

Grace had a brilliant idea as she stepped onto the wooden planks for a closer look. Her imagination took over, *"What an incredible idea. If I play my cards right, this is a once-in-a-lifetime opportunity to see the Tahiti Islands from the unique view of a small seaplane."*

Her eyes sparkled with delight as she stopped beside him. Now she hoped her French was good enough to communicate to him that she'd like to go up in the seaplane. *"I've got nothing to lose, so here goes!"*

"Prenez-vous des touristes pour les rides?" *Do you take tourists for rides?*

"No," he answered with a laugh. *"Boy, I never saw that coming,"* he thought in surprise.

"Personne n'a jamais demander de monter avec moi," he continued. *"No one has ever asked to go up with me."*

"Tout le monde semble peur de mon petit avion," he replied. *"Everyone seems afraid of my little plane."*

"J'apprends à voler, j'ai toujours voulu essayer un petit hydravion," Grace proudly explained. *"I'm learning to fly a seaplane. I wanted to go up in a small plane."*

She thought with delight, *"This will be a perfect way to view the French Polynesian Islands."*

"Comment avez-vous obtenu ce plan ici," she asked? *"How did you get this plane here?"*

"Je me suis envolé cet avion tout droit de France! Il m'a fallu un certain temps, mais j'ai adoré." *"I flew this plane all the way from France! It took me a while, but I loved it."*

"Eh bien, je serais ravi d'aller en elle. Je serais heureux de vous payer!" *'Well, I would love to go up in it. I'd be happy to pay you,'* Grace said hopefully.

The man didn't answer immediately as he contemplated what he'd do. *"This was not only highly unusual, but since I was on the lookout for people that don't add up, this young lady is highly suspicious and someone I should keep my eye on."*

"Oui! Mais je dois travailler jusqu'à 14:00 aujourd'hui." *'Yes! But I have to work until 2 pm today.'*

"Merveilleux! Je vais vous rencontrer ici à 14:00. J'attends un appel depuis mon domicile à 17:00, donc qui va s'intègrent parfaitement."

Grace clapped her hands in joy as she exclaimed, *'Wonderful! I will meet you here at 2 pm. I expect a call from my home around 4 pm, so that will fit in perfectly.'*

Grace felt like she was on cloud nine as she strolled back to the resort, *"This is even more wonderful than I ever imagined."*

"Oh, there's the manager," she thought as she entered the atrium. She was beaming with joy as she approached him with her exciting news. And practically gushed, "Hello, Mr. Allaire, I've arranged with the young man down by the dock to go up in his little yellow seaplane at around 2 o'clock."

"What?" exclaimed the man in alarm. "No one goes up in that bucket of bolts!"

"Well, I asked him *special*. It's a perfect way to see the islands, so I'm thrilled."

"This is unbelievable, Madame! Philip is always repairing and tinkering with his plane."

"Oh, I understand. I just wanted to check if it would be safe to go up with *Philip*. Is he a good man? I hope my French was good enough so that he understands that I want to return here!" Grace explained as she pointed to the resort. "I told him I'm expecting a call from home about 4 pm, so I'll need to be back by then."

At this, the manager stated with caution, "Well, … Yes, Madame, Philip is very safe. It's his plane that I'd be afraid of."

"Oh, no worries there. I'm sure it will be fine."

He nervously laughed as he admitted, "But, Yes! Our Philip is a fine young man and perfectly harmless."

Grace smiled with satisfaction as she turned to leave. She realized how lucky she was, *"Wow, I've just secured one of the most unexpected treats of my whole trip. I've got ample time to add a few things to my Adventure Kit, which had to be stored safely inside my checked suitcase for the flight. For instance, my Swiss Army Knife with 20 attachments. The airlines are careful about what they allow in carry-on luggage.*

"Now let's see, I'll need my binoculars, and I'll need to charge my phone for pictures. Maybe I'll freshen up with a quick shower."

Grace spotted a brochure rack in the lobby and paused to check it out. *"Great. Here's one about the Venus Pointe Lighthouse!"*

She looked further, chose another one that showcased an idyllic picture of paradise, and read, *"The Islands of Tahiti, French Polynesia, are a collection of 118 islands and atolls. Many of the islands still remain uninhabited."*

She couldn't bypass the stunning brochure that featured the private, over-water bungalows in Bora, Bora. *"Boy, these are some of the most romantic accommodations in the entire world."*

"I think I'll also take this booklet, a historical review of French Polynesia." As she flipped through the pages, she frowned, *"This also gives information that is not so positive as it describes the explorers' impact on the islands.*

"The sailors introduced many diseases to the islands for which the islanders had no immunization protection. The impact of these initial interactions with explorers had devastating consequences for the Tahitian population, which dwindled rapidly, afflicted by diseases."

Grace thought about the similar circumstance of the American Indians brought on by the explorers and early settlers in Eastern Canada and America during New England's Great Dying!

The parallels are undeniable!

One of the last flyers she saw was *Famous People Associated with Tahiti!*

Paul Gauguin (1848-1903) - De rin Paris-born Gauguin is, among other things, the creator of romantic images of the South Seas.

Sir Joseph Banks (1744-1820) - Banks was an English botanist and naturalist with James Cook on his first trip to the Pacific, including Tahiti. Coming from a wealthy family, he had financed half the expedition cost of Cook's trip. The other half came from the British Crown, by the way.

William Bligh (1754-1817) - Bligh is known to many as the captain of the Bounty, which is known to have led to a mutiny against him. The mutineers under the second officer of the bounty, Christian Fletscher, then ended up on the small island of Pitcairn. After the mutiny, Bligh achieved the maritime masterpiece of reaching the island of Timor from over 3,600 nautical miles with a number of followers after a journey in an open dinghy – in which the mutineers had put him.

Bligh set sail from England on December 23, 1787, and reached Matawai Bay on Tahiti on October 27, 1788. He was supposed to take plants of the breadfruit tree on board and bring them to England. Because of the wind conditions (monsoon), he was only able to leave Tahiti on April 5th of the following year. In the course of the trip, the mutiny mentioned above took place on April 28th.

Marlon Brando (1924-2004) - In 1960, Marlon Bando from 'The Mutiny on the Bounty' in Tahiti. In 1962 he married the Tahitian Tarita Teripia.

In 1990 Marlon Brando's son, Christian Brando, kills his sister's lover in Tetiaroa. The sister committed suicide five years later and was buried next to her lover on the islands. The ashes of Marlon Brando, who died in 2004, are said to have been scattered on Tetiaroa.

Jacques Brel (1929-1978 The Belgian chanson singer came to Hiva Ora on his yacht in 1975 and decided to settle there. In 1978 he died of cancer in Paris – where he had gone for treatment – and was later in Atuona on the Calvary Buried cemetery not far from Gaugin.

Captain James Cook (1728-1779) - The navigator and explorer James Cook is especially famous for his three voyages of discovery to the Pacific region. He has discovered or visited numerous islands. On his third voyage, he was slain by natives in Hawaii. The leading destination of his first trip to the South Seas from 1768 to 1771 was Tahiti to observe the so-called Venus transit on the occasion of the solar eclipse of June 3, 1769, in order to obtain data for calculating the distance between the earth and the sun. The astronomer Charles Green and the botanist Joseph Banks were also on board.

Johann Reinhold Forster (1729-1798) - Forster was a German natural scientist and ethnologist. He first studied theology in Halle and worked as a pastor for a while. But his genuine interest was primarily in science. After studying and researching in Russia, he went to England with his son Georg in 1766, where he had already made a name for himself as a natural scientist. From there, he accompanied his son Georg on James Cook's second trip to the Pacific. The ship set sail from Plymouth, England, in June 1772 and returned to England after a three-year voyage. From August 17 to early October 1773, the ship and its crew stayed in Haiti.

Charles Green (1735-1771) - British astronomer Green accompanied James Cook on his first South Seas voyage to Tahiti to collect data from Venus's transit on the solar eclipse of June 3, 1769.

Jack London (1876-1916) - the American writer and author discovered the fascination of the South Sea islands during his Pacific voyage from 1907 to 1908, which he carried out with his sailing boat "Snark." Impressed by the exoticism of the islands of Tahiti, he wrote the "Stories from the South Seas."

Herman Melville (1819-1891) - In 1842, the American writer Herman Melville deserted to the island of Nukuhiva. There he spent several weeks – together with sailors from the whaler "Acushnet." He describes his impressions there in his novel "Taipi," published in 1846. In his book "Omoo," published in 1847, he told about his experiences in Tahiti. His travel experiences also inspired him to write the world-famous book "Moby Dick."

Tupaia (1725-1770) - priest and navigator who accompanied James Cook on his first voyage to the South Sea in 1769 and, among other things, served as a translator.

Chapter 7

Meanwhile, at the Sea Crest Lighthouse, Michael paced back and forth nervously while watching his brother James navigate the crumbling jetty leading up to the lighthouse. "Good morning, James," he called out.

"Hi. I got your secretive message that you wanted to talk with me. What's up?"

"I need to get your opinion on an idea I have," stated Michael slowly.

"I'm all ears, but let's climb up to the top landing and take advantage of the view."

"Okay, but let's grab some coffee," replied his brother happily. He stepped over to a nearby counter and pushed the heat button on the Keurig. Shuffling through the coffee pods, Michael asked, "Have you tried these coconut ones?"

"Yes, they're delicious if you add cream," answered James with a smile. "That was one of Grandma Chamber's favorites."

They finished fixing their coffees, went up to the balcony, and looked out over the Sea Crest area. They reflected on their good fortune as they took in the scenic waves crashing along the beach.

The view from the top was interrupted by James's question, "Did you want to see me for something special?"

Michael began earnestly, "Yes, "Something Special" is what I need. I've been going over in my mind all the plans and effort you went through to make sure Maggie could keep Misha. You designed a perfect way to give her the most meaningful gift in her world."

"Oh! I just did what had to be done," stammered James. "It would have broken Maggie's heart to lose Misha! Anyone would have done the same!"

This outburst completely silenced Michael as he reasoned, "No one else could have dreamed up the series of events that you used to make it happen, my dear brother!"

James' voice broke as he whispered, "Michael, you should have seen her one night while we were in the Underground Railroad. I woke up in the middle of the night. After re-orienting myself to the fact that we were underground, I looked through my goggles to find her sleeping beside me." As an afterthought, he whispered in amazement, "She actually looked like an angel."

At this point, Michael couldn't think of one thing to say as he contemplated, *"We've never had a conversation the likes of this before."*

James realized he couldn't dwell on the lump developing in his aching throat as he continued, "I saw her goggles lying beside her and reached to pick them up. They were soaked. She had fallen asleep crying! Can you believe it? Something had to be done. Michael, I couldn't stand it!"

After a moment, Michael asked, "Was that when you realized how much you truly cared for Maggie? The first time you saw her as vulnerable and not the confident, no-nonsense FBI Special Agent you were constantly fighting?"

"Well, truth be told, after reading Grandma Chambers' letter, I'd begun to feel like Maggie wasn't so bad after all. She was more of a worthy adversary. You know - more admirable, much better!"

Michael agreed, "Yeah, almost likable."

The brothers finished their coffee, and James said, "We are the two luckiest guys I know. How blessed are we to have married these two wonderful friends?"

Michael explained earnestly, "That's exactly why I need to talk with you. I want to ask your advice on a surprise for Kate. I'm thinking of taking a page out of your book on this."

"What do you have in mind?"

"Pugs! My Kate loves dogs, and she's especially attached to Misha. She told me this is the first time her family hasn't had a current dog at the Sea Crest keeper's cottage. She said it's strange; however, since Misha is there a lot, she feels better."

James agreed, "Oh yes! Kate has mentioned how much she loves all breeds of dogs."

"Well," added Michael, "She even told Dad and me that the U.S. Coast Guard primarily trains explosive detection dogs and beach patrol.

"Kate, as a US Coast Guard SARS helicopter pilot, has been part of their helicopter training for the past few years. These dogs are called 'Canine Coasties,' They wear protective goggles and ear devices to guard them against rotor wash, spray, engine noise, and debris."

"Now, I didn't know that!" James laughed. "But when you mentioned Pugs, did you remember Jack, Grandma's breeder in NYC? She got dogs from him over the years, and he's saving a pick of the litter puppy if we'd like it. Jack is associated with the American Kennel Association in New York. Grandma was an avid supporter and board member for many years.

"He is aware that Grandmother Chambers has passed away, but she had contacted him a while back and told of her desire to get another short-nosed pug puppy. Jack said the puppy is old enough, and his papers are in order, so he's ours if we want him. He's headed down here to Sea Crest later today on business, and he can bring the puppy down if we'd like him."

"Boy," exclaimed Michael. "That offer is timely, isn't it?"

"It sure is," agreed James. "We grew up loving the comical, affectionate pugs as our family pets. Although Grandmother Chambers did not have one during the last year of her life in New York City. She has delighted in their companionship and love for most of her life."

Michael joined in, "I vividly remember Grandmother telling wonderful pug stories. They revealed that in its native China, it was the lap dog of preference for numerous Chinese emperors.

"He chuckled as he continued, "It seemed that our dogs knew she was bragging about them as they'd hop up on her lap or get cozy next to her as she talked. Their little wrinkled face was looking up at her intently."

Both Jensen brothers looked out over the water, remembering their past.

Michael boldly stated, "Well, I miss Grandmother, and I feel that having this little guy around would be a treat. What should we name him?"

"Oh, not to worry. Grandma already named him. She told Jack: Sir Snarfs-a-lot. Rhymes with Sir Lancelot. Nickname - Snarfy."

Chapter 8

"Not to change the subject, but isn't it crazy what Kate found in the cornerstone?" Michael asked James.

"Boy, you can say that again! To think that Robert Louis Stevenson actually touched that note and put another note in the Tahiti Lighthouse cornerstone, referencing the connection to Captain James Cook's ancestry," answered his brother.

Michael was quick to add, "Yes! Simply amazing, isn't it? As an architect whose business specializes in lighthouses all over the world, I can tell you a little about how important these cornerstones are to historic buildings. During our lifetime, they've been hollowed out and filled with timely letters, clippings, pictures, and meaningful items, related to the purpose of the building. The inscription engraved on the stone usually included the completion year of the structure.

"Of course," he continued, "most cornerstones include coins, metal, currency, stocks, and other things of monetary value. However, here are some other buildings and statues that are different. For instance, some civil war statues have had two cornerstones hidden in the monument's pedestal.

"Well, I hope Grace can unravel the location of the contents of the Tahiti cornerstone. She was so excited. Oh, that reminds me; I'm supposed to contact Attorney Jeffrey Williams in New York. I need to see if he'll be available to supply some research for Grace at this end if she needs it. He offered to help her on various historical research projects when you and Kate had your wedding celebration."

"Sure. Why don't you call him now?"

"Okay," James said as he stepped over and dialed his number.

"Hi Jeff," this is James Jensen, and I'm here at the Sea Crest lighthouse with my brother Michael.

"Well, hello! I was just wondering what they found in the lighthouse cornerstone."

"That's what we're calling about," James answered. "Grace found a sealed note from Robert Louis Stevenson inside. She explained that his family was the famous Scottish Stevenson Lighthouse Dynasty of builders for over three hundred years.

"His father, Thomas Stevenson, built the Venus Pointe Lighthouse in Tahiti to honor Captain James Cook in 1868. That was around the same time our Sea Crest Lighthouse was built by Sir Michael Chambers and the architect Joseph Walsh."

Michael said, "Grace thinks James Cook's family ancestors in Great Britain were friends with the Chambers family of Scotland."

"Wow! That's amazing," Jeff marveled.

"Well, it gets better," continued James. "Robert Louis Stevenson's note explained that the Tahiti lighthouse cornerstone held an unopenable locket with pictures of Captain and his wife, Grace. The special key that opens the locket will be passed down thru the future ancestors of the Cook Family. When the cornerstone in the Tahiti Lighthouse is discovered, the one who possesses the key will prove their relationship to Captain James Cook."

"Long story short, Grace is on her way to Tahiti to discover if the cornerstone was ever found during the 1965 repair of the lighthouse. If so, what happened to the contents? There are two museums near the lighthouse, and she thinks her family might have the old Victorian key that opens the locket."

"You're kidding!" exclaimed Jeff.

"Grace asked us to see if you could do some research for her if she needs it. You probably have access to much more information that she'll have available."

"Oh, nothing would give me greater pleasure. I'd love to help Grace."

"I'll let her know when she calls from her resort," said James.

"Fine. Where is she staying?"

"I think she's planning to stay at The Tahiti Hilton. It's brand new and near the airport. She'll move closer to the lighthouse and museum after she starts investigating."

"Okay, I'll keep in touch. Bye for now," Jeff signed off. However, he was already busy pulling up the next flight to Tahiti. *"Let's see… I can leave this evening and connect through San Franciso, California. I can be in Papeete, Tahiti, by midnight tomorrow.*

"This is just the opportunity I've been wanting."

He picked up the phone and dialed a direct-line number from his business contacts.

The call was answered after two rings. "Hello, The Captain James Cook Society. How may I help you?"

"Hi, this is Jeffery Williams. I need you to forward some of the files to me on the 1965 repair of the Venus Pointe Lighthouse in Tahiti!"

Chapter 9

Grace took a curious look inside the cabin of the yellow seaplane and thought, *"It's strange that Philip has such extensive equipment installed. I've flown a small plane with only two seats quite often, but it didn't have all this technical stuff."*

As a pilot striving for her seaplane certification back home in Sea Crest, Grace silently observed, *"Yes, the basic equipment is similar. But I remember that when international pilots communicate with the air traffic control towers where they fly, they speak English. In fact, English is used all over the world. There will, however, be cases where a pilot may not speak English, like Philip. Then it's up to them to constrain themselves to airspace where they can click the radio to use a language they speak."*

Philip's vintage seaplane was a Piper J-4 Cub Coupe that was introduced in 1939. It featured a door on each side and a wide fuselage that accommodated a side-by-side seating arrangement. Many of the Piper Cub models, like the J-3, had tandem seats.

Grace smiled and cheerfully paid the agreed-upon money she had offered to pay him for the sightseeing flight. Philip put these bills in a separate part of his wallet, *"Later, I will check these bills for fingerprints and serial numbers. They may be from a recent bank robbery. Maybe even part of the Albert Spaggiari heist, for all I know. He was the mastermind behind the biggest-ever bank robbery in France, and he died, leaving no clue as to the whereabouts of the stolen millions. It's believed that he had help from someone on the inside. This lady is a cool customer and could easily pull it off."*

She was just a little too happy for his liking. Philip felt an unreasonable desire to burst her bubble of good cheer.

He viewed her knapsack with suspicion, "Qu'y a-t-il dedans?"

'What's in that?'

"Oh, just my camera and stuff," she replied innocently. "Oh, juste mon appareil photo et tout le reste."

He reached for her backpack, asking, "Combien ça pèse?"

"How much does it weigh?"

She handed it to him, thinking, *"it's probably heavier than he expects with my Adventure Kit hidden safely inside. You never know when you'll need something incredibly valuable that could save our lives!"*

Philip heaved his toolbox into the back, declaring sarcastically, "Pour la chance!"

"For Good Luck!"

Philip accessed the surprising weight of her backpack. He balanced it with his tool kit when he positioned them to safely ensure the stability of the seaplane.

Before taking off, Philip stated, "Je montrerai comment utiliser les préservateurs ou les vêtements de flottaison individuels (VFI) pour chacun d'entre nous à bord."

"I will demonstrate how to use the preservers or personal flotation devices (PFD) for each of us on board."

He then demonstrated where to find and remove it from stowage and its packaging, how to put it on, inflate it, and when. "Cependant, NE JAMAIS L'INFLAIRE DANS L'AÉRONEF !"

"However, NEVER INFLATE IT WHILE IN THE AIRCRAFT!"

Grace nodded her agreement. She remembered from the recent paperwork she read while preparing for her seaplane lessons, *"Various dangerous goods or hazardous materials are illegal on board a seaplane. These include gases, corrosives, spray cans, flammable liquids, explosives (including ammunition), poisons, and magnetic materials."*

Grace shifted in her seat as she fit the seat belt snuggly around her hips and clicked the shoulder harness into place. Then, out of habit, she found and released the latch with both hands, with her eyes closed until she was sure she could do it in an emergency.

Philip watched this procedure and recognized, *"Yes, this strange lady is something else. She may be carrying drugs in that backpack, but she's familiar with professional emergency escape techniques."*

As an afterthought, he laughed inwardly, *"I guess in case of a crash, I'll rescue the drugs first."*

Grace showed Philip two colorful brochures. The first one showed The Point Venus Lighthouse. *"Pouvons-nous aller à ce phare?"* *"Can we go to this lighthouse?"*

Philip glanced over and nodded yes.

She held up the second brochure about the bird sanctuary on the island of Tetiaroa and asked, "Apouvons-nous aller à la réserve d'oiseauxbout?"

"Can we go to the bird sanctuary?"

"Oui! Je le sais bien !" *'Yes! I know it well!'*

Philip happily thought, *"Tetiaroa hosts a pristine environment, and the atoll is part of the*

natural reserve. Apart from the fantastic beaches, you will encounter incredible wildlife both

under the water and in the air.

"With limited ways to get to the island of Tetiaroa and the lighthouse, the best way for normal visitors is to join a weekend

cruise departing from Papeete or charter a boat. This is the first time anyone has asked me for an aerial view in my seaplane."

Philip put on his headphones and handed her a pair. He spoke into his microphone and began advising the tower that his intentions were to stay within the airspace of French Polynesia, both departing and returning to the Papeete Airport, today. His conversation about his flight with an air traffic controller was French. Flying in controlled airspace around large airports, you must advise the controllers of your intentions and follow their instructions. You don't need a pre-filed flight plan, but you are under their control and need permission to be in the airspace. This helps in places like (PPT), Papeete Airport, where the airspace gets busy.

Grace was silently amazed, *"I can't get a visual of how close we are to the Papeete Airport, but that's who he must talk to. I'm also aware that although they speak French, the international language of aviation is English. In most places, the pilots and air traffic controllers have demonstrated the ability to speak and understand English up to a level specified by the International Civil Aviation Organization (ICAO)."*

Philip turned the ignition and slowly turned the seaplane toward open water. Grace felt an incredible breeze sweep through her hair as the seaplane gathered speed and rose out of the water. She felt free as a bird as the small plane's pontoons lifted out of the clear blue water. *"Boy, this is living! I will never forget this exhilarating feeling of excitement for the rest of my life,"* she pledged to herself.

As the seaplane gained altitude, she watched the beautiful Tahiti Hilton Resort as it faded away beneath them. Ahead of them lay a beautiful expanse of over 140 tropical islands and atolls.

As they progressed, the islands of Tahiti continually unveiled their spectacular beauty. Grace had flown along the Sea Crest coastline many times, but this scenery was very different. This turquoise ocean was dotted with lush islands, tall waterfalls, and plentiful beaches. The color of the sand ranged from pure white to pale pink to dramatic black.

Many of the island's volcanic rocks had produced jagged, irregular coastlines. Some islands had sheer cliffs rising out of the jungle, featuring waterfalls cascading down to the aquatic pools below.

Grace reopened her bird sanctuary brochure. She quickly read as they approached Tetiaroa. '*It shelters one of the largest colonies of birds in Tahiti and her islands. These include white terns, brown boobies, frigate birds, red-tailed tropical birds, and the amazing, great crested birds. Their colony is the only one in the Windward Islands.*'

As Philip pointed to the fast-approaching island, Grace pointed and yelled, "*Le voilà !*"

'There it is!'

"Merveilleux!" She exclaimed as the tropical birds came into view. Grace immediately took out her cell phone and took some of the most stunning pictures of her life.

'Wonderful!'

"Oh, Wow!" Grace declared in amazement, "On dirait que nous sommes sur le point d'entrer dans une grande formation de nuages blancs."

'*This looks like we're about to enter a large white cloud formation.*'

"Oh non!" Philip cried. "*Bird Strikes! He had heard stories about the damage and fatalities caused by birds like these large White Sea Birds from the Bird Sanctuary.*"

The seaplane plowed straight into the massive flock of squawking White Tern Birds, generating thousands of white feathers and body parts. The cockpit looked like a colossal pillow fight gone awry.

Philip's hands were cramped as he fiercely clutched the steering wheel, trying to right the small aircraft. The seaplane lurched sideways, causing Grace's high-pitched scream to resound throughout the airspace and crashing her cell phone into several flying projectiles. The last piece was clutched in a dying bird's claw as it plunged into the ocean. Without missing a beat, a large dead bird knocked her headphones off her head and landed, still flopping, in her lap.

"Help!" she shrieked with an ear-piercing cry, trying to shove the horrible bird off her legs.

The smashup that ensued involved several birds taking turns as they crashed headlong into the engine. Yes, you guessed it. The engine stopped. The bent propellors left the plane awkward to steer.

He yelled loudly to Grace, "Nous ne voulons pas être échoués en mer. Aidez-moi à chercher une surface de plage plane avec une chute d'eau en vue."

'We don't want to be stranded at sea. Help me look for a level beach surface with a waterfall in sight.'

As the plane lost altitude, the bent propellors left the plane awkward to steer. It was not stable enough to glide smoothly or turn correctly. However, Philip made a heroic effort to direct the aircraft close to one of the islands with a visible beach area.

Grace yanked all the feathers and debris away from her face and wildly grabbed her binoculars from her backpack. She held the lenses up close to her eyes. However, she couldn't see anything with all the jiggling movement and the birds fluttering around in various degrees of survival. Her vision was so obstructed she thought she'd get a clearer view by looking out the side of the plane. But it was too late!

As the seaplane hit the water, Philip bellowed, "Hold On!"

Chapter 10

Michael held the new puppy in his arms back in Sea Crest as they watched the vehicle drive away. "That's right, Snarfy, wave goodbye to Jack. You are the big surprise he just dropped off to complete our new family."

The dog whimpered softly and wagged his tail.

"Don't feel bad; just wait till Kate sees you. She's going to flip!

"In fact, we are going to call her right now."

The puppy laid his head in the crux of his arm as Michael dialed Kate's mobile number.

As she picked up, the puppy nodded off to sleep. "Hi Kate. Are you busy right now?

"Well, I just finished a surfing lesson. What do you have in mind?"

Michael laughed, remembering that's where he first met her. "Well, I'd love to see your finishing act again!"

"Well, just so you know," she responded, laughing as well. "I'm still embarrassed that I was shamelessly showing off for you like that! I'll never live it down!"

"And just so you know, I'll never forget it! What are you doing right now?"

"I was going to stop at the house and grab some lunch. In fact, I'm almost there."

"Great, so am I. We can order pizza. Bye."

Michael hurried to the bathroom, put a fluffy bath towel down on the floor, and gently laid Snarfy in the middle. Next, he returned to the living room, collected all of the puppy's things, and arranged them around the sleeping dog. *"What a sweet little bundle of joy."*

When Kate arrived, he was hanging up the phone from ordering a large pepperoni pizza with extra cheese.

He greeted her with a kiss, "Hi, I just ordered our favorite pizza."

"Thanks, I missed you today. Every time I give surfing lessons, I'll miss you sitting on that bench watching me ride that terrific wave back to shore."

"Don't you worry," said Michael. "The memory of what I saw you teach that day is definitely etched in my mind for all eternity. And here's another thing: none of the girls you were giving those surfing lessons to could hold a candle to what I saw you do that day!

"I love thinking of all the special memories we've made since we met. Today I was also remembering memories of my grandma Chambers. I miss her so much."

"I know you and James both miss her terribly."

"Do you want to know something about her that I've probably not told you yet?"

Kate put her hand on his cheek and looked into his eyes as she nodded and kissed him.

Michael explained, "Lately, I've been thinking about my grandmother Chambers and recalling many poignant memories about her. Since we were young when our mother died, many of my early thoughts revolve around things that a young boy would value."

"I can agree with that line of thinking. I'd love to share those memories with you."

Michael explained, "My grandmother always had adorable small, short-nosed pug dogs as far back as I can remember. They were very precious to her and offered untold comfort to me. I vividly remember Grandmother telling wonderful pug stories revealing that in its native China, it was the lap dog of preference for numerous Chinese emperors and their wives."

He chuckled as he continued, "It seemed that our dogs knew she was bragging about them as they'd hop up on her lap or get cozy next to her as she talked. Their little wrinkled face looked up at her intently.

"Pugs were introduced to the United States after the Civil War. The breed was recognized by the American Kennel Club in 1885. At first, Pugs were very popular, but by the turn of the century, interest in the breed waned. A few dedicated breeders kept breeding, and, after some years, the breed regained popularity. Our grandmother Chambers was very involved with the New York Chapter. That's where she met a breeder named Jack, who became a special friend of my grandparents."

"That sounds like a wonderful part of your childhood, Michael."

"It was grand," he said. "Of course, as an adult, my work kept me constantly moving from place to place. It wasn't a good option to consider having a pet. But now," he smiled as he reflected on the memories, then softly added, "Well, I miss my grandmother, and I feel that maybe having a little pug-nosed puppy around would be a treat."

Kate thought she would burst with love for him as she agreed, "Yes, that would be wonderful!"

"I'm glad you agree because Jack was on his way down here this afternoon on other business," explained Michael as he took her hand. "He called to let us know that Grandma Chambers had asked for the next 'pick of the litter,' and he could bring it today if we wanted it," Michael said nervously. "Do you think it's too soon to add to our family?"

"It sounds wonderful!" cried Kate as she kissed him with joy. "What should we name it?"

"Jack said Grandma already named him Sir Snarfs-a-lot. Rhymes with Sir Lancelot. Nickname - Snarfy."

At the sound of his name, a small puppy wandered into the room. Snarfy had toilet tissue wound around his head, through his mouth, and stuck to his front foot.

Kate cracked up. "Well, hello, Snarfy," she laughed.

Michael called, "Come here, boy." With that encouragement, the puppy came running the rest of the way out of the bathroom with a three-foot trail of toilet paper flowing behind him.

As Kate lovingly picked him up, tissue and all, Michael happily asked, "aren't we just the luckiest people in the whole world, Kate?"

Chapter 11

Grace and Philip's emergency landing on the water was far from ideal. The plane was moving fast when multiple birds struck and stopped the engine. Since Philip was an experienced pilot, he could keep the nose pointed above the horizon for a long enough time for the plane to glide and slow down for a short time.

The steering was also hard to turn because the wheel was bent and crooked. By the time the plane hit the water, it had done a fair amount of spinning around in circles at high speed, but thankfully, it did not flip over.

Philip headed the nose of the plane toward the nearest island as soon as it stopped rotating but still moving nicely. The rising tide should help get them close to it.

He looked over at Grace and asked calmly, "How are you? Are you hurt anywhere?"

She answered, "I'm fine. Are you hurt?"

When he answered that he was alright, she asked, "Why didn't you tell me you could speak perfect English?"

He didn't answer for a long time and acted like he was concentrating on coaxing the plane toward the island.

After a minute, Grace asked, "Do you want me to use my backpack as a paddle? It's waterproof, you know."

He found that very strange if she was carrying drugs in it. Maybe even a gun or weapon of some kind. "How do you know it's waterproof? What's in that thing anyway? It's very heavy!"

"Oh," Grace announced proudly, "It's my Adventure Kit!"

"What?"

"You know, it's like my Survival Kit, everything to keep me safe. My Mah Jongg friends all have them."

"This I gotta see!"

"I'll show everything to you later." Grace paused, "Right after you explain why you are fluent in English."

'Oh Boy, Now I'll have to think up something believable.' After a minute, he said, "Well, it's part of my job. The resort doesn't want me talking to the guests. By the way, I think we're close enough to land to get off and pull the seaplane ashore."

"Okay," Grace said as she jumped into the knee-deep water.

"Wow, I didn't expect that!" he thought as he stepped out of the other side of the cockpit into the water. "I think the first thing we need to do is secure it, so the tide doesn't let the plane float away when it rises and surrounds it."

Grace smiled as she agreed and asked, "Do you have any kind of a rope or bungee cord in your toolkit?"

"Yeah. Let's see, we can drag it onto the sand and secure it while we try to repair it on land. How does that sound?"

"Fine. Do you think we can secure it to that low-hanging coconut tree?"

They worked together, dragging the plane over the sand and tying it in four places to anchor it to the tree. Philip was pleased with the seaplane's position as he explained, "Yes, this is great. We can reach the propellor and the engine to work on them."

Grace asked, "Do you know where we are?"

Philip looked at her and shrugged, "Not really. I tried to get a good look from the air, but I'm pretty sure it's not Marlon Brando's Island where they are building an up-and-coming high-end Eco-Hotel/ Resort."

Grace leafed through her brochures, found the resort he was talking about, and began reading aloud. "The Brando is a unique luxury resort on French Polynesia's breathtakingly beautiful private island of Tetiaroa – an atoll composed of a dozen small islands surrounding a sparkling lagoon 30 miles northeast of Tahiti. The Brando offers carefree luxury amid pristine nature. With access to the island by private plane, the resort features 35 villas on white-sand beaches frequented by sea turtles, manta rays, and exotic birds. The resort was designed to reflect Polynesian lifestyles and culture."

Philip agreed, "Yeah, that sounds like it. I know it's near the bird sanctuary where we had this Bird Strike, but I don't think this is it. I'll bet this is uninhabited. Hopefully, I'll get these crazy scrambled birds out of this engine and straighten the bend in the propellor before nightfall."

"What can I do to help?" asked Grace.

He pulled his toolbox out of the seaplane. He handed Grace an assortment of needle-nose pliers to help remove all the bird feathers and debris caught inside the engine. "We must be careful not to further damage any parts, so be careful as you go."

He explained, "I'm going to use a coconut for a brace and try to hammer out this bent propeller."

Grace laughed, "Hey did you see the movie 'Cast Away' when Tom Hanks' character survived a plane crash and was stranded on a desert island?"

"Of course, everybody saw it."

"Good! Remember how he struggled to crack open coconuts before finally figuring out how to tap into one and drink from it? Well, not to worry, Philip. I know all about coconuts! I've got that covered."

Philip turned and rolled his eyes as he sarcastically said, "Well, good luck with that skill-set. Hopefully, we'll have this 'baby' up and running in about half an hour. But you're welcome to bring back a few with you to the resort," he offered. "Knock yourself out!" he chuckled as he shook his head. *"She's probably going to pull a gun out of that backpack and use them for target practice."*

As it turns out, about a half-hour later, his baby was not even close to '*up and running*.'

Chapter: 12

Philip looked at his watch and measured the setting sun's angle against the ocean skyline. *"There is no way I'll be able to get this seaplane repaired before dark."* He contemplated how to break the news to Grace. *"How will she react?"*

Grace saw the worried look on his face and asked, "Well, how does it look? What's the plan?"

He hesitated as he looked long and hard at her, then decided to tell her the truth. "We can't get this seaplane running before it gets dark. I think we should make a plan to prepare, find food and make a shelter as quickly as possible."

Grace turned to see the colorful red-orange wash over the sky and paint the most beautiful sunset she'd ever seen. It touched the ocean's edge as the sun slowly descended its glowing path. She wistfully made a ludicrous statement, "Yes, but did you ever see a sunset this amazing? It takes my breath away!"

As an afterthought, she added, "Yes, I'd be happy to crack some coconuts to eat, and I know how to weave the palm branches for shelter."

Philip's mouth hung open a little too long, and Grace started suggesting what 'HE' could do now! "Oh Philip, could you cut some of those bamboo stalks growing over by those bushes? I think about 8 feet long will work best. Then I'll show you where to cut out a section on one side, allowing the bamboo to be bent at a

90-degree angle. We can make a great bamboo and palm leaf shelter in just a few minutes."

Philip was shocked at her delight in the situation. "How do you know about making a shelter out of bamboo and coconut palms?" he asked suspiciously.

"Oh, I saw it on YouTube! My friends and I were making our survival kits, and we watched a video all about it. In fact, that's where we made sure that if we were ever stranded on a deserted island, we'd be prepared."

Grace continued, "This is one of my favorite Amelia Earhart quotes: *'Preparation, I have often said, is rightly two-thirds of any venture.'*"

That made Philip smile as he challenged her: "My favorite quote is *'Flying might not be all plain sailing, but the fun of it is worth the price.'* I've often thought that Amelia would have loved my little seaplane."

After a moment, he solemnly pointed out, "You know her plane went down in the Pacific Ocean. That's the same body of water where we are flying. However, I'm sure we have much better odds of being rescued, even if we can't get this plane going. Amelia said she was running out of gas near Gardner Island, which we now call Nikumaroro. I recently heard that they might have found her plane. They are now testing the bones of a woman with new forensic methods. These were unavailable when those remains were first discovered."

Philip sighed, "I always thought she looked like Mia Farrow."

They worked in silence, getting the bamboo set up as the bent framework for the shelter and a bottom layer for the base, where they could sleep.

Grace mentioned, "YouTube also informed us that bamboo is grass. So, like your lawn at home, it not only grows super-fast but also regenerates when it's cut. What we've cut today will grow back without replanting it. But it's best to leave space between the

49

various stalks of bamboo, so we don't disrupt the local eco-system, affecting plant diversity and disturbing animal habitats."

"That is what makes it eco-friendly by design," stated Philip. "I wish that concept applied to all the forests harvested annually worldwide."

They soon finished their shelter but knew they had much more to do before dark.

Grace asked, "Do you think we should make a fire next?"

"Yes, if we can get it going while we still have time to gather something to burn."

"Well," Grace said, "I have matches in a moisture-proof container. I believe coconuts have a very burnable layer of fibrous husk before we get down to their hard shell. It looks like wiry straw, and we'll save all of it. I'll gather some driftwood, and we'll soon have a great fire."

"Wow! She's really into this survival stuff," thought Philip. *"I'd better count my blessings."*

Before gathering wood, she wove a huge palm branch into a lightweight mat. When she folded it in half, it made an excellent basket-type carry-all. She returned with her new basket full of various kindling before she offered to open several coconuts to eat. Now, Grace was going to really shine. She laughed as she picked up her survival kit and said, "Get ready, Philip. I will impress you with one of my favorite Christmas presents."

"Oh no," thought Philip. *"This is where she'll pull out the drugs!"*

She opened her backpack and removed her Swiss Army Knife with 22 attachments. "This knife is 'all' I wanted for Christmas a few years ago."

"You wanted 'that' knife?"

"Yes, This exact one. It's the Swiss Army Knife: Victorinox. Not all Swiss Army knives were created equal; this one is special on many levels! It's made to help you survive and live in many situations.

"The Swiss Army Knife designer Elsner renamed his company, Victoria, in memory of his mother after she died. The "inox" suffix comes from the French term you might be familiar with, Philip. It's acier inoxydable, meaning stainless steel. The combination spells Victorinox. These models are considered the true Swiss Army knife."

"You don't say! I've just met an expert in Swiss Army Knives," he chuckled as he shook his head.

Grace smiled as she told of how lucky they were to have landed on this island, which was abundant in coconut, bananas, and bamboo. She explained, "We'll be in fine shape! The people of the Pacific refer to the coconut palm as the *Tree of Life*. It's known to have a thousand uses, and it's the tree that provides all life necessities. If you were stranded on an island like we are tonight, I've heard that you'd want to be blessed with a mature coconut tree for company. There are stories about island and coastal people in the tropics surviving months of drought with coconut palms providing the only drinking water available.

"Just look at all these coconut trees. They're great for both coconut milk and coconut fruit. These trees won't look like those with a brown fuzzy shell in a grocery store. These have a hard green surface surrounding the brown shell. Some will have no water if we collect the ones on the ground. Shake them and listen to check if you hear water inside. The ones that are full of water are up in the trees. They'd be the best if we have access to them," she finished proudly.

After a second, she continued, "Of course, all coconut trees are palm trees, but not all palm trees can produce coconut!"

Philip just stared at her, *"Who is she anyway? An advertising executive or lobbyist for the coconut industry?*

Grace didn't skip a beat as she continued with her information in a lesson on how to crack coconuts. "You just pull out this Phillips-head screwdriver and stick it in one of the three eyes on the top of the coconut."

She quickly poked a hole in the top of four coconuts. "Now, let's get that collapsible cup out of my survival kit." She quickly poured the coconut water from the first one into it and set it aside.

"Next, we can use a rock to pound the hard shell along the crack as it opens until we break the shell in two. Now we can extract the coconut pieces with my knife," she finished, handing him a refreshing piece of moist coconut.

"Now we have two cups. If you have a file in your toolkit, we can make the edges smooth so we don't cut our mouths."

After successfully executing these steps, Philip and Grace drank the sweet coconut milk from their new coconut cups. Grace had a couple of more surprises as she shared her supply of Acidophilus pills with Philip. "These are advised for travel, especially to tropical destinations, but they might help you also. I know you live here in Tahiti. However, while on this island, your body might negatively react to the foreign water that is not treated like your resort purifies their water. Web MD advises starting these pills 3-5 days before the trip and continue for 1 week after we're home for best results."

She handed the container to Philip, who read aloud, "These Acidophilus Probiotic + Prebiotic Supplements are for Gut Health. 31 Unique Strains. For Men & Women. High Potency 50 Billion Live Cultures. Thanks! I appreciate these."

Philip looked at the fading sunlight and suggested, "I think we should take a quick look around for a stream or waterfall. I didn't see any fresh water source when we ditched here. However, it could have been concealed by the trees and lush vegetation."

Grace chimed in, "We definitely don't want to drink the ocean water. Not only is the salt in ocean water dangerous, but it also contains many pollutants like oil, fertilizers, pesticides, and trash. These pollutants can cause you to become very sick and even die."

He explained, "They advise: If you have to drink ocean water because you're lost at sea, ensure that you have removed the salt. To do this, you will have to use an enclosed container to evaporate the ocean water. This removes the water from the salt. After the evaporation, condense the water into a separate container. Do you have anything like that in your "Adventure Kit?"

Grace opened her backpack, pulled out a special water bottle, and said, "You mean something like this?"

"Yes," Philip answered with a laugh. "Exactly, if that purifies water."

"Well, yes and no," she proudly announced. "It purifies, not desalinates. This has an all-inclusive system that filters and removes all pathogens for up to 65gallons of water per replaceable cartridge. It's a complete answer to purifying drinking water in any natural disaster, water emergency, or survival situation.

"However, where the issue of ocean water is desalinated to make it into drinking water, we're not quite there yet in a convenient 12 oz bottle. I know that the mega cruise ships have Fresh Water Production Plants on board which can turn three million liters of seawater into drinking water daily. They provide more than 80% of all freshwater used on the ship. We don't have anything for the smaller volume we need on a portable scale yet."

"However, I might have an answer we can try for tomorrow if it makes sense to you and it's not too strenuous. I think I saw a small stream or the possibility of water as the sun made a ribbon of shiny silver on the side of a hill. I wasn't sure of anything except that we were dropping in a free-fall this afternoon. The stream might be just over that cleared area, running down that hill," Grace pointed out.

"Great," said Philip. "That should be fresh water. If it's cool enough in the morning, that might be something we should check out before we work on the plane. We can use your pills to ensure it's safe to drink."

Grace agreed, "Yes, and let's set a limit on our search time and effort so we can have the energy to work on the seaplane. Of course, we can still use the plentiful coconut milk to keep hydrated."

"That's wonderful!" Philip smiled and then continued. "As I look over our progress today, I was concerned that we would expend too much energy and risk exhaustion. We need to pace ourselves while trying to prepare ourselves for safety and survival."

"I vote for a small rest while we take in the beauty of this picturesque aqua water before us. The rhythmic tides almost lull one into a trance as you gaze at these simmering clear ocean waves," Grace wistfully noted.

As they agreed to pause and enjoy the scene for a bit, Grace commented, "Speaking of waves, do you think the tides here are always this calm along this shore?"

Philip quickly replied, "Now you've touched on something I know about! Tahiti is 99% water, so much of our life revolves around it."

"Well, I've heard about great Hawaiian surfing, but I haven't heard much about the French Polynesia Islands," she replied.

"Let me tell you about the famous, or infamous, surf break known as Teahupo'o. After we get my seaplane repaired, I promise to fly you along the south coast of Tahiti, where we can view the world of big wave surfing from the air. Several times a year, elite athletes gather as monster swells form along the horizon and grow into the planet's most unique and previously "unrideable" waves.

"I had some Tahitian friends that used to come to the North Shore of Oahu every season and surf in the Pipe Masters," Philip recalls.

"Those guys had always talked about when Teahupo'o 'does its thing,' it's a sight to behold. Unique seafloor topography, and the shallow reef on which the surf crashes team up to create a wave unlike anywhere else on Earth. Whereas many big waves are tall and thin, the waves at this Tahitian reef appear as thick as they are tall, increasing the wave's power exponentially.

"Well, Laird Hamilton, arguably the greatest surfer of all time, heard about the mysterious Teahupo'o back in the 1980s from visiting Tahitian surfers. They tried to convey the ferocity, energy, and danger of a wave that was mythical amongst locals. Years later, Hamilton finally gave in and traveled to Tahiti.

"He was amazed as he studied the power of the waves. The surfers were pulled onto the wave by a Jet Ski, known as tow-in surfing, to catch the monstrous rolling waves as they swelled. That day, Laird Hamilton rode a once-in-a-lifetime tubular Tahitian blue beast. He produced one of the most famous rides in surfing history on August 17th, 2000. Now it's simply known as the Millennium Wave.

"You can view the whole ride on YouTube.

"That's amazing," replied Grace. "I have a friend who is a champion surfer. I can't wait to tell Kate of this super wave along the southern shore of Tahiti!"

"I'll bet she knows all about Laird!" Philip said proudly. "The ride he completed that magical day will forever be immortalized in images, videos, and firsthand accounts. It had the most significant impact on the surfing community by re-establishing what was rideable and opening the minds of countless other surfers.

"Right now, Foiling (or surf foiling) is the hottest sport in surfing, and it's at the forefront of almost all ocean pursuits. It's basically riding a surfboard with a hydrofoil attached to the board instead of a fin. This allows the surfboard to fly above the water. The surfer is essentially surfing the foil but riding the board," he happily concluded.

After a sigh of relief, he looked around and said, "I guess building our fire is next on the agenda."

Philip watched Grace pull out her waterproof container with the matches inside. He smiled and said, "I'm so glad you have those! It sure beats trying to start a fire by hand no matter how much coconut fiber we have!"

"Yes, this tin is full!"

Grace and Philip worked together to build a fire circled with rocks.

Grace suggested, "Do you think we could make the letters for S.O.S. just encase someone is searching for us early tomorrow before we're up and around?"

"Yes, we could make giant letters in the sand for tonight. Tomorrow we'll probably just need help if we haven't got the seaplane repaired yet. "

"Okay," agreed Grace. "We could print out: HELP & Aidez-moi!"

"How about Emergency & Urgence!" added Philip. "Yes, we should print out HELP if they see the fire tonight! Do you think anybody even knows we're late?"

"Oh my," Grace remembered. "I was expecting a call at the resort hours ago."

While Philip was picking out a few nice rocks, he noticed an editable fruit that was tasty growing along the woods. "Hey, look! Wild pineapples," he exclaimed. "The town of Moorea is northwest of Tahiti and is known as the pineapple center of French Polynesia. That area has a mix of volcanic soil, which is ideal for producing the majority of Queen Tahiti pineapples. Pineapples are believed to be native to South America and were then spread across the world via British and Spanish explorers. The first record of pineapples in Tahiti dates back to 1777 in British explorer Captain Cook's voyage log. Today, Queen Tahiti pineapples are available in local markets in French Polynesia, especially in Tahiti and Moorea.

"A juice factory mixes pineapple juice with other local fruit juices for retail. It is one of the significant sources of income for the people of Moorea. They also have an annual pineapple festival with fresh fruit tastings, wine, and traditional dishes.

"These are growing wild on this island, which is another excellent food for us." He took a knife and cut a chunk off. "Here, try this!" as he offered her a bite.

"Wow, very nice!"

"If you get a chance when we return to the Tahitian Hilton, they serve one of the best dishes cooked in an ahima'a. That's an underground oven."

"What else do they cook that way? Is that like a pig roast I heard about?"

"Yes," he answered. "The resort has several weekly events. They come up with delicious recipes for Polynesian ovens, where fruits, vegetables, suckling pigs, Tahitian chicken fāfā (local spinach), and other delicacies."

"We should either get the seaplane going or get rescued sometime tomorrow, so we should be fine," said Philip positively.

Chapter 13

Joe could hardly wait to hear her voice as he eagerly dialed the number of the Tahitian Resort. He happily reflected on the fun they had both delighted in as they manipulated James and Maggie into falling in love.

At least, that was how they saw it.

"That's right! We'll take full credit for the two falling for each other," he reasoned. *"Furthermore,"* he continued. *"The thrill we shared was hard to beat as we planned and plotted for these two sworn enemies to be continuously flung together, clashing every step of the way.*

"Why, I've never felt so close to anyone. I couldn't wait to be in the presence of my co-conspirator. Of course, it was all in fun. Just friends! Nothing serious between us at all.

"Well, that's not to say I didn't have that one strange reaction to that New York City lawyer trying to dance with her at Kate and Michael's wedding celebration. He was definitely out of line. Grace needed protection from this playboy type, so I had to cut in and rescue her. I know he has many wealthy New York City clients, and I'm sure he thought he could dance with anyone he chose."

Joe suddenly heard the desk clerk at the Tahitian Resort pick up his call, and he responded eagerly, "Hello, I'm calling for your guest, Grace Cook."

"Oh, the resort manager will be right with you, sir."

"No…, please, Ms. Cook is expecting my call this afternoon."

"Yes, I understand, but I need to put you on hold. The resort manager, Mr. Allaire, asked to talk to you as soon as your call came in."

A bad, apprehensive feeling overcame Joe as she put the call on hold.

He remembered the alarm he had experienced earlier upon hearing that Grace had packed and boarded a flight headed for French Polynesia.

This unsettled feeling was a new experience for him, that's for sure.

Joe's phone call was taking a little longer than he'd expected.

It was slowly dawning on him that she was not only a close friend. But also a growing realization that he missed her and possibly genuinely cared for her.

The resort manager's worried voice interrupted Joe's train of thought as he spoke into the receiver, "Hello. I understand you are calling for Ms. Grace Cook?"

"Yes," answered Joe. "What seems to be the problem? Is Grace all right?"

"Well, ah…, see…, here's the thing," stammered Mr. Allaire. "We expected them back over an hour ago."

"You expected my Grace back?? I'm calling for Grace C O O K. She's waiting for my call," explained Joe.

"Well, she said she'd be back in time for this call. They must have been delayed."

"Wait a minute, where did she go?"

"Well…, I'm not sure exactly," he hesitated. "They went in his little yellow seaplane at 2 o'clock. She was very excited and asked Philip if he'd take her up for a ride in it."

"What? Who is Philip? Does he take guests up for sightseeing tours?"

"Ah, no. This is the first time anyone has ever agreed to go up in that little seaplane. She asked him. Said she was taking flying lessons and wanted to know if her French was good enough for him to understand that she wanted to come back here."

"What? Who is this guy?"

"Sir, Philip is a young Frenchman who works here. He loves that little plane and works on it all the time. He's perfectly harmless. We're just worried that they haven't returned yet."

Joe was feeling more and more scared with every word he heard. He shouted, "Have you called the authorities yet, to report this …, ah…, kidnapping?"

With that, the unnerved manager blurted out, "It's nothing like that! We figure it's a problem with the plane!"

"Really? Do you think they crashed? Okay, you give me the ID information on this guy right now. I'm going to have the FBI run a check on him."

Mr. Allaire was quick to admit, "the only thing on his resume was that he was an adventure-seeking type of male model who had apparently excelled in soccer. Philip might have played on Spain's World Cup Soccer team, but we never checked it out. He does have a striking resemblance to Antonio Banderas, and that alone is good for business."

The emptiness that Joe had felt upon hearing that she had flown halfway across the world without him was now replaced with a rush of fear that he was losing her. Not only physically losing her, as in that Grace was missing, but the full-fledged agony of pain that he had waited too long. Why didn't he recognize love when it was right in front of him?

The manager finished the conversation by writing down Joe's contact information and promising, "I'll call you as soon as we know anything."

Joe was ready to lose it as he practically shouted, "Wait, I'll be arriving on the next plane. But, rest assured, Grace better be there safe and sound!"

As Mr. Allaire heard the phone receiver slammed down in his ear, he sadly thought, *"Yes, I know what you must feel like. One of my last memories of the Love of my Life was putting our 'Love Lock' on the Pont des Arts Bridge across the Seine River in Paris. It connects the Institut de France and the central square of the Palais du Louvre. We met and feel in love at the University in Paris. She was a talented art student, and we spent hours at the Louvre.*

Her family was against our love, and when they heard that we planned to marry, they packed her up and pulled her out of the University. My heart was broken. I searched for her for years, but I never saw her again.

Chapter 14

Meanwhile, the young Frenchman who worked at the Tahiti Hilton Resort was lying in the homemade bamboo/coconut palm shelter, wondering just who Grace really was. *"Why is she carrying all these survival supplies? Did she somehow sabotage my plane and know my plane was going to run into that flock of birds and end up here? Why did she want to ride in my seaplane? Let's see: she had the brochures for Tetiaroa Bird Sanctuary, which shelters one of the largest colonies of birds in Tahiti and the Point Venus Lighthouse."*

Before he had an answer to these questions, he heard Grace whisper, "Philip, are you awake?"

He thought about pretending to be asleep but thought, *"I'd better try to find out all the information I can about her."*

"Yes, I'm awake," he said.

"Do you know you look like Antonio Banderas?"

"Yeah, I get that a lot!"

"Well, are you related to him or something? Are you his twin brother?"

"No," laughed Philip. "However, I did have a job as his stunt double for the Zorro movies: *The Mask of Zorro* and *The Legend of Zorro*. That was where I learned and perfected my talent as a swordsman."

"Wow! How exciting is that?" Then Grace laughed and told him, "You know, my best friend, Mary Beth, has an unhealthy obsession with everything concerning Antonio Banderas!"

"Really? What does she do?"

"Oh, she's way over the top about him. She knows all the songs on the Evita soundtrack.

"Yes, learning the latest apparatus used in fencing competitions was enjoyable. Did you know that the Olympics have used electrical and electronic technology to score points for a long time?"

"No," answered Grace. "What are you talking about?"

"Well, the fencers wear vests that conduct electricity. This creates a complete circuit through the fencer's sword point and back to the ground. The pressure breaks the circuit when that point touches the vest, and the electronic system knows a point was scored."

"Wow, I didn't know that."

"The first patent was filed by two people from Ohio on Mar. 25, 1974, and granted on November 18, 1975, known as Electrical Fencing Scoring Method and Apparatus. Different points were given for various hits. The apparatus produces visual and audible scoring signals in response to valid and invalid touch signals produced to execute valid and invalid touches with a fencing weapon."

"That's amazing!"

"I know! I was obsessed with the whole process and studied how it all happened. I got to learn and practice with Antonio. That was another special gift."

"Oh," he continued, "That was how I got the gig as his understudy in *Evita*. That was a blast. Of course, I had to take dance and voice lessons."

"You've certainly had an exciting life because of your looks.

They silently listened to waves for a few minutes until Philip asked earnestly, "Now can I ask you something?"

Grace was still processing Philip's newfound Star Power as she said, "Yes, of course."

"Well," he asked innocently, "Are you related to MacGyver?"

Grace was so tickled that she replied, "Yes, just call me *Mrs*. MacGyver." She laughed and explained, "I've just been hanging out with my Mah Jongg buddies for too long. We play every week, and we are the best of friends. We are all about safety and learning to take care of ourselves, and we just *live* for this stuff."

"They sound like a fun bunch of friends!"

"Yeah, they're the best. When making our Survival Kits, we followed what we called MacGyverism to get the most bang for our buck."

"Okay, I'll bite. What is MacGyverism?"

"When you're a guy like MacGyver, you get the pleasure to swap which model of Swiss Army knife you carry. From 1985 to 1992, MacGyver's most used knife was the Tinker by Victorinox. The Tinker has 12 functions and weighs 62 grams. It's the perfect tool to tinker your way in or out of a tricky situation. In fact, the 12 functions have served us well."

"Just encase I need to know them for Jeopardy next week, what are they?" Philip laughed.

"I thought you'd never ask, but we get to share the money you'll win. These are in no particular order: large blade, small blade, Phillips screwdriver 1 – 2, reamer, punch, and sewing awl, can opener, screwdriver 3mm, bottle opener, screwdriver 5mm, wire stripper, key ring, toothpick, and tweezers."

"Well, that should get you plenty of help with many things. I'm duly impressed."

"So were we. We also liked the story behind the name and the fact that it was dedicated to his mom, Victoria."

Philip said, "I've been amazed by your "Survival Kit" and safety knowledge."

Grace smiled and thought, *"It's surprising that a guy would complement me like that. I'm glad I made such a good first impression."*

After a few more minutes, Philip broke the silence as he asked, "Now, will you please explain who you are and what you're doing here in Tahiti?"

Chapter 15

The ordinarily laid-back, easy-going Joe was in a full-blown anxiety attack when he reached FBI Special Agent Maggie O'Hara.

"Maggie, did you know that Grace went to Tahiti?"

"Why yes, she came by on her way to the airport," she happily replied. "We had scheduled a Mah Jongg game, but she couldn't stop to play. However, we made up this little 'Adventure Kit' for her to take with her. It was a scream! Why, what up?"

"She's missing," Joe blurted out.

"What? No, she must be in Tahiti by now."

"Yes! She did arrive. However, she went up in a seaplane with some strange Frenchman, and they never returned."

"Okay, Joe, calm down. Tell me exactly what happened."

As he repeated his phone conversation, Maggie typed it into her FBI database. She had worked on several international cases and had contacts all over the globe.

She also knew that Kate was off for the next three days. She was a Coast Guard Search and Rescue Commander, and she'd bring expert help if their friend had crashed.

"Okay, Joe. Kate and I will see what we can do."

Maggie finished pulling up all the available information on her computer and asked for the photo of Philip. *"Oh no! This is not good,"* she gasped. Wrong name, but she found herself looking straight into the eyes of someone she knew very well!

Chapter 16

"Who do you think I am?" laughed Grace.

Philip definitely was not expecting her answer. "Granted, I didn't check your ID or passport before I let you on my seaplane, but I'd really like to know. For the record, I've changed my opinion every time you open your "Survival Kit.""

Grace thought about that for a minute and said, "I'm Grace Cook. I'm a historian looking for information from the cornerstone of the original Pointe Venus Lighthouse, which was repaired in 1965. It might connect my family to Captain James Cook's family."

Now it was Philip's turn to laugh as he said, "I almost believe you. Nobody could come up with a cover story like that! What an imagination!"

"Hey, I'm not kidding. Why wouldn't you believe me?"

"What makes you think, in your wildest dreams, that you could possibly be related to Captain James Cook? And make it good!"

"It's probably not true, but I have to find out! I was processing the contents of the cornerstone of the lighthouse in the town where I'm the Town Historian. I found a rolled-up document with Robert Louis Stevenson's seal. It spoke of something special that his family, The Stevenson Lighthouse Dynasty, had placed in this lighthouse to honor the future family of Captain James Cook's family."

The hair on the back of Philip's neck was practically standing-on-end at this strange news. *"What am I supposed to do now?"* he thought. "Okay, I believe you," he said. "Now go to sleep!"

The exciting day finally took its toll on Grace. She felt totally drained as she turned over to go to sleep. That's when it hit her; *"I wish I was sharing this adventure with Joe. Over the last couple of years, he's been my best friend. I can't believe how much I miss him. I haven't talked to him today, and it's been months since we've had a day that we didn't talk at least once."*

She sadly thought, *"This feels strange. I wonder what Joe thought when he called the Tahiti Hilton Resort today, and I wasn't there. They didn't know we'd had that bird strike damage the seaplane's engine. I'm sure the hotel manager figured we were just delayed, and Joe will call tomorrow."*

Chapter 17

Joe Lawrence was not having a great morning! He hadn't slept well all night and was feeling the results now. *"I don't know what I'll do if something's happened to Grace. Why didn't she let me know she was planning to go to Tahiti? Oh, that's right, I was in court all day yesterday. Well, be that as it may, she could have waited until today, and then I could have gone with her. Then she wouldn't have gotten into that seaplane with that guy."*

"Really now! Who actually looks like Antonio Banderas? I'll bet Antonio Banderas doesn't even look like him. He probably has a team of hairdressers and stylists working round the clock on him. To say nothing about the trainers trying to get him into shape. And I'll bet this imposter has never even been to a World Cup Game, to say nothing about playing soccer in one. Poor Grace is way too good for the likes of him. She's halfway around the world, and who knows what has happened to her."

This ridiculous banter has been happening since he called the Tahiti Hilton Resort.

"I'm almost packed, but I still need to contact an attorney who will substitute and handle my case while I'm out of town."

He made the call to his associate, who was going to fill in for him. "Hello, this is Joe Lawrence. I have an emergency I need to handle, so could you please stand in for me and handle my court case today?"

"Yes, sure. I can move a couple of things around, no problem."

"Great, I can have my staff prepare my case documents and outline how I want to proceed today and in the future. I'm going to be out of the country. I might be gone for a whole week."

"Is there anything else I can do for you?"

"No. Just handle this case. I appreciate it!"

"Well, if you want anything, just let Grace know, and we'll help with anything you need."

Joe replied sadly, "Grace is the one who's in trouble…, She's missing!"

Chapter 18

The first Sea Crest person to follow Grace to Tahiti was Mary Beth. As soon as she'd left Grace off at the airport, she had immediately gone home and packed her bags to take the next day's flight. That happened to be an overnight flight. The following morning she arrived in Tahiti and checked into the Tahiti Hilton Resort. Of course, she asked, "What room is Grace Cook in? I'm a close friend, and I wanted to surprise her."

A very stressed-out reservationist gave her the room number but said Grace Cook was out at the moment. "Oh, that's okay," Mary Beth replied. "I'm going to catch up on my sleep. I love that Hilton offers the special Tempur-Sealy line of Hilton Mattresses known as the Luxurious Exclusive Hilton Collection. I can't wait to relax and test it as I fall asleep. I'll see her later."

A few hours later, Sarah and James Cook's flight connected through San Francisco and arrived in Tahiti. The resort manager took over at this time to let them know, "Your daughter is out, but I'll let Grace know you have arrived."

They told the manager they had jet lag and needed to lie down for a while. "We'll see her later."

The manager called the authorities and reported both Philip and Grace as 'Missing Persons.' The FAA called the tower to check on the flight plan that was filed by Philip. None was available. However, a suspicious incident was reported in which an entire flock of white tern birds was hit. A trail of feathers and dismembered bird parts were scattered throughout the entire Tetiaroa Bird Sanctuary Tetiaroa Bird Sanctuary.

The workers reported to the authorities, "Our whole island was disturbed, and the birds and wildlife reacted to this terrible commotion. This was supposed to be a refuge and safe haven for them, and now there was chaos and mayhem. The dead body parts seemed to be most distressing for them. Nearly all birds display aggressive behavior and make plenty of screeching noises when perceiving a threat. This was pretty violent, and we expect those responsible should be held accountable."

The authorities answered solemnly, "Yes, we promise to get to the bottom of this. We have a couple of possible suspects that may have some connection to the incident you described."

"Well, we hope so."

"We'll keep in touch. Goodbye for now."

Chapter 19

Joe finished his packing, his third cup of coffee, and locked up his house. *"Now, I've got to get to the airport and catch that flight!"*

He drove to the airport and circled the parking lot for what seemed like an eternity. Finally, a space opened up, and Joe parked and practically ran through the parking lot to grab a shuttle to the airport. At last, Joe was inside the main terminal. A few minutes later, when he promptly threw his bags on the conveyer belt to get them scanned, he heard a loud resounding clang.

He was shocked to look down at his luggage and see his small duffle bag. He always kept it in the back of his car as a mechanical first aid kit. It was a small toolbox and included a few rolls of the ever-popular duck tape, a hammer, a screwdriver, pliers, and twelve-fifteen tools.

The baggage checker heard the loud jangle, unzipped the bag, and inquired, "Sir, just where do you think you're going with these items?"

As another TSA Agent came over to see what violation this passenger was guilty of, Joe explained, "Oh, I didn't realize I'd collected this with my other bags. I keep it in the trunk."

"Please come with me, sir!" the TSA agents instructed.

"No, you can have the tools," Joe protested. "I didn't even know I had picked them up."

"Sir, please come with me!"

The two TSA agents herded Joe into another area, where they each put on a fresh pair of gloves as they asked him, "Sir, are these your bags?"

"Yes, of course, they're my bags."

"Did anyone give these to you or ask you to carry them for them?"

He answered, "No." But he was thinking, *"Yikes, now I get where this is going."*

"Were they out of your possession at any time?"

"No."

"Please unlock your bags and take a seat, Sir."

"I have a flight to catch," Joe said.

"I'll bet you do. However, we have a job to do. We have to figure out why you're carrying a bag full of tools, many of which are over seven inches long. This airline does not allow these tools in your carry-on luggage." The agent signaled his fellow ATF officer and stated, " We are also very curious about what you plan to do with all this duct tape."

"Nothing special. It was kind of a joke when a couple of my friends gave it to me as a gag gift. We always found it amusing that everybody tries to fix everything with it."

"Well, we found nothing illegal unless you carry it on the flight. For this flight, you'll need to check your tool kit with your checked luggage."

"Thanks," said Joe as he left the private area and proceeded down the terminal to the gate.

"Hey, where is everybody," he thought. He glanced at his watch, *"I can't believe it! I missed the flight!"*

He searched a nearby sign showing the next departures for Tahiti. *"Oh, No! There's not another one until tomorrow evening. It won't arrive in Tahiti until ... the day after tomorrow."*

Chapter 20

The following day when Grace woke up, Philip already had the coffee on. Since coffee beans grow wild in Tahiti, he just had them steeping in hot-boiling coconut water over the fire.

She smiled with pleasure to wake up on this beautiful tropical island. "Wow, isn't this just the best? It's like a dream come true!"

"Yea, I hope your dream includes fixing the seaplane so we can get off this island. Here, I made coffee," he stated as he handed her a cup.

"How did you make coffee?" she asked as she smelled the sweet aroma.

"I had to boil the coffee beans in the coconut milk. Do you use cream and sugar?" He laughed as she nodded, "Well, this is the best coconut latte you'll ever have."

"We've had wide varieties of coffee growing wild since they were introduced to the islands in the 1800s. Tahiti now grows it commercially with great success due to the favorable climate and volcanic soil. I even threw in a few vanilla beans to make it taste perfect. That's another one of our exports."

Grace happily commented, "This is delicious! Isn't it a miracle that so many things grow wild here?"

"Of course, but we still should take our trek to discover that waterfall you thought you spotted yesterday. I noticed the wind had picked up this morning. I want to get any strenuous exercise done early and reasonably. What do you think?"

"Yes, I think that's the best plan. The better prepared we are with good drinking water, the better off we'll be, no matter what happens. If we get the seaplane repaired quickly before lunchtime, we'll be back at the resort by my folks' arrival." She thoughtfully added, "They are coming to help with the investigation about Captain James Cook's family ties."

They quickly prepared the coconut cups and purification pill and headed toward the incline.

Philip noticed, "This walk across the clearing is a little further than it looked. I think I can make out the winding waterfall up on the hill."

"You're right. I couldn't judge the distance where the silver ribbon was shining like water when the sun hit it yesterday, but I think it's ahead too."

They climbed a little further, and sure enough, there was a small stream.

"Now, let's test out this water," he said as he dipped his cup into the stream and then dropped a pill.

They waited like two little children waiting for the magic to happen. When the water tested "drinkable," they laughed as if they'd just invented fresh water! They happily toasted each other with their first cups of clean water from the freshwater supply.

"This is delicious!" marveled Grace. She casually strolled over to get a good look at things from a higher altitude. She pointed her binoculars toward where they'd camped last night, and as that area came into view, she screamed, "Oh No!"

Philip promptly swung around to see his little yellow seaplane drifting out to sea!

Chapter 21

The following day, Mary Beth called the front desk and discovered Grace was not on the hotel premises. On her way down to get breakfast, she ran into Grace's parents in the lobby. Grace's mom hurried over to her and asked, "Oh, Mary Beth, have you seen Grace?"

"No, not yet" Then, seeing their distress, she added, "Why? What's wrong?"

"She went out for a sightseeing ride with a young man in his seaplane, and they haven't been seen since yesterday afternoon. They are both missing!"

Grace's Dad added, "We just talked to the manager. He said a man named Joe Lawrence called Grace yesterday afternoon when he got out of court. He said Grace had left a message that she was expecting his call and would be back in plenty of time for it. The manager told Joe that Grace left with a guy named Philip who had a seaplane, and they never returned to the resort as planned. Joe was very upset and said he was on his way here, and Grace better be here 'safe and sound.'"

They all turned around as another familiar face walked into the lobby. Mary Beth said, "Hey, Jeff Williams, aren't you the Jensen family's attorney?"

"Yes, I'm looking for Grace. She asked James to contact me and see if I could help her with some research on Captain

James Cook. Since I'm on the Captain James Cook Society in New York City board, I thought I'd come down and help her in person."

"Well, she's missing!"

"What?"

"Yes," explained her Dad, "She went on a sightseeing ride with a seaplane guy yesterday afternoon. They have not returned."

The manager stepped up to inform them, "We are organizing a search party. French Polynesia covers about 140 islands and atolls, stretching over 1,200 miles in the South Pacific Ocean. Many of these are uninhabited areas."

James Cook asked, "Where should we look for them first?"

"Luckily, we had a waiter leaving the elevator who saw Grace Cook taking some brochures out of the rack. He said it looked like Grace was most interested in the Pointe Venus Lighthouse and the Tetiaroa Bird Sanctuary. I left messages at each of these tourist offices to see if they've seen or heard of any yellow seaplane in the area. They should be opening up and getting back to me in the next 15 minutes."

Sarah Cook asked, "Will the search be by air or water?"

The Manager explained, "French Polynesia is also fortunate to be under the safety umbrella of the United States, COAST GUARD ACTIVITIES FAR EAST (FEACT). They have many resources at their disposal, including a Coast Guard Hercules aircraft – plus a Dolphin helicopter. However, it appears that Grace has some important friends on the way. One is a US Coast Guard Search and Rescue helicopter pilot, and the other is an FBI Special Agent. Since they are experts in this field, we welcome their help. They have agreed in advance to take the lead on this search."

"Great! That must be Kate and Maggie," shouted Mary Beth, as she clasped her hands over her heart with joyful hope!

The manager ran his hand through his hair nervously, "There is also an attorney named Joe Lawrence who was very upset last night when he called to talk with Grace. He is threatening to bring a legal lawsuit and sue the resort and everyone

80

else here in Tahiti if she's not safe and sound by the time he gets here."

"Yes," Grace's dad nodded in dismay. "I know; Joe is normally very level-headed in most instances. However," he whispered, "He'll be a powerful force to be reckoned with if anything bad happens to her. He's no doubt the one who's bringing the top rescue people from the United States along with him."

As an afterthought, he looked Mr. Allaire in the eye and added, "Boy, you'd better be sure she's okay."

James took his wife gently by the arm and privately acknowledged, "Dear, I'm pretty sure Joe's in love with our daughter, and I'll bet she feels the same way. I just don't know when it will dawn on them."

Sarah agreed, "Yes, I've noticed how close the two have grown. I see the laughter and camaraderie they share. I can't tell if it's friendship or love. Only time will tell."

Chapter 22

Grace and Philip started running down to the campsite until Philip advised, "Wait! We need to conserve our energy." They quickly powerwalked to their shelter.

"Wow, look at how high the tide is! We might have just discovered how the seaplane got loose," Philip marveled as he looked at the coast.

"What do you think happened?" asked Grace.

"Look at these water levels. When the tides rise at Teahupo'o on Tahiti's south beach, the big surfing waves rise up all along the beaches of nearby islands in French Polynesia. This island must be near enough to Tahiti's huge surfing waves that this tide was also affected. The waves rose high enough that the seaplane we had secured close to the shoreline was swept away."

"The seaplane is now out of reach, but I wonder if it will come back near our beach as the waves and tide calm down and things return to normal. That's a chance we'll have to prepare for. We need to create a rescue signal if we hope to be saved. It will help search parties find our location faster. We'll do what we can to be safe today, but we know we should send a signal for help. Grace, do you have one of those signal mirrors in your survival kit?"

"Yes, but I'm not 100% sure how to set it up. Let's see; The instructions claim that it's a flash that can be seen for up to

100 miles. The signal mirror has been called the most underrated survival tool in a survival kit," she answered with pride.

"My friends and I did watch how this works on YouTube, so it should be easier to follow these instructions.

"Let's see, first, reflect sunlight from the mirror onto your hands or some other nearby surface

"Next, hold the mirror up to your eye, extend your other arm and form a V with two fingers. This is a front aiming sight.

"Third, place the mirror reflection and the target in the front sight (V).

"Last, slowly move the mirror back and forth. Continue sweeping the horizon even when no search and rescue craft is visible. The idea is to tilt the signaling device back and forth toward whatever target might pick it up: a passing plane, helicopter, boat, or someone on an inhabited body of land. In other words, anyone who can help you.

Philip added, "I heard three stranded men were rescued after a passing ship noticed a flash on the distant horizon. The flash was from a signal mirror hanging from an unconscious man's neck.

"Military survival kits must include a signal mirror, and all personnel are trained to use one. "

Grace reminded him, "Well, the YouTube video made it simple for us to see how to set up and use a signal mirror. We should also move it back and forth or hang it from a twig in the sand for better coverage.

Philip added, "Yes, I have an Aviation Emergency Kit in my seaplane, which includes a signal mirror. However, I've heard that even a side view mirror could save your life in case of an automobile accident. Use anything shiny reflecting the sun's rays, like a canteen or belt buckle for a signal mirror."

Grace looked at him seriously and asked, "Have you ever had to use that kit from your seaplane?"

"No, but I've seen the pilots ask if there was a doctor on the flight. I'm not 100% sure, but I understand that medical professionals, like good samaritans, who voluntarily provide emergency medical assistance on a commercial aircraft are protected from liability."

After a moment, he continued, "We should also plan for the nighttime, so we should prepare a signal fire this evening. We need to have round-the-clock signals. The smoke signal is the best way to get the attention of passing planes or helicopters in the daytime. That's how the Boy Scouts are still taught and how the Native Americans did it."

Grace chimed in, "Let's not forget the earliest lighthouse locations were often fires which served as a warning to ships. These early visual signs of danger saved many lives through the ages.

Philip added, "We can produce a lot of smoke by burning damp wood. We'll start with dry coconut coir or fiber. Then we can add more wet driftwood to make the smoke appear. If the wood is too dry, we can sprinkle some water to moisten it."

Grace asked, "Do you know the international signal for HELP when it comes to fire? It is three fires in a triangular formation or three in a straight line about 80 feet apart. I think the wind has died, but we must be cautious about spreading the fire to nearby woods around us."

Philip agreed, "Great idea. I think we have room to build the three fires in a line. It's probably easier to manage to keep the smoke visible this afternoon. I believe loading wet palms on the fire might effectively create the thick white billowing smoke. We can dip the palm branches in the ocean and see how that goes," he said.

They got busy with the fires and soon had all three smoking up a storm.

Philip was amazed, "Wow, this white smoke that can be seen for hundreds of miles. Toss me that old jacket we retrieved from the seaplane last night to throw over us. We have a much better use for it now, to signal the S.O.S. Now how should we do this?"

"Well, I'll bet it would make a signal if we wet the jacket fabric, then cover the fire for about a second and pull it off three times in a row!"

"Yes," agreed Philip. "We can't disturb the fire too much. It should send three separate puffs of smoke into the sky, which is the international signal for trouble. Then we can move to another fire in our triangle and repeat the signal."

"That sounds right. We should re-wet the jacket with each new fire. Rinse and repeat style," Grace said as she brought him a freshly doused jacket.

Philip gladly took it and gingerly arranged it over the fire. Then he quickly yanked it off, sending a billow of smoke into the air. "You realize, of course, that if you hadn't 'Insisted' on going for a ride in the seaplane yesterday, we might have missed this once-in-a-lifetime opportunity to execute all these survival technics for our real survival."

"Boy, we're enjoying this way too much," Grace laughed. As she shaded her eyes and looked out to sea." she said, "Hey, your seaplane is way out there! But I hope it comes back near this beach when high tide comes in tonight."

"I wish we had a scarf or something big we can wave if we see a search and rescue helicopter or a boat out in the water," said Grace.

"How about those coconut palms? They are big enough to see from afar and don't weigh much," speculated Philip.

"Wow! That's the perfect answer! And they are growing everywhere."

Philip suggested, "Yes, now let's sit down and rest. We've done much work today and still need to conserve energy."

"Sounds good. I've gathered some pineapples and coconuts to munch on!"

Suddenly, Grace ran toward the waves, screaming and laughing, "Look at this!"

Philip followed her to the beach's edge and bent to pick a little yellow rubber duck out of the water. "I know what this is from," he laughed. "I've seen a couple of these over the years."

"You've got to be kidding me! I can't believe this toy just came in on that wave! How can that be?"

"Well, I know exactly all about it," stated Philip. "Now, I'll give you two guesses to figure it out!"

"Oh, come on. I think it's impossible, but I'll try to come up with a logical explanation! First, give me a clue," challenged Grace.

"I already did. The first clue is, I've seen this before."

"Really? What's the second clue? No, wait, I'll ask a question you have to answer about."

Philip nodded his consent.

"Okay, I want to know if you expect to see one again?..... Wait, Part two of this question is, Does this happen anywhere else?"

Philip thought for a minute while he inspected the rubber duck and finally said, "I'm always surprised by these and love the sheer pleasure I feel when one appears. For the second part, these can seemingly appear from out of nowhere, at odd places."

Grace admitted, "I guess I'm stumped. Is this some kind of special Tahitian prank you can somehow play on tourists?"

"No, but that's a great idea. I remember 1992 when I first saw the newspaper headlines. They called the event Moby-Duck. The article explained how 28,800 bath toys were 'Lost At Sea' when a cargo ship hit a hurricane. The container broke open when it tumbled into the North Pacific, dumping 28,800 toys into the ocean."

"The toys were originally shipped from China (Big Surprise). These ducks have been washing ashore in Scotland,

Alaska, Japan, Hawaii, the western coast of Canada, the United States, and various countries for years. They think at least 2,000 remain at sea in circular currents in the ocean called 'gyres.'"

"Wow!" said Grace. "I've not heard of that before."

"Okay, Grace. Have you ever watched those science shows on TV? In this case, these toys are hollow and have air inside. The shape is constructed with a smooth shell-like surface. No potential openings. There are no caps to fly off or seams to split open, so they just float endlessly around the world until they land somewhere on a beach. Some of the beachcombers who first found them have been working with oceanographers, tracking the various ocean currents, for years. Artic researchers discovered that many of these toys were caught in the polar ice caps for years. When they emerged and continued to float around the world, they were found in pristine condition. No paint damage at all."

"Wow, that's incredible!"

"Books have been written about the event and where these toys ended up," Philip ended.

Grace thought, *"What a great example of all the surprising things people have never even heard about. This awesome worldwide scavenger hunt involves people from all walks of life. Most never knew where the rubber toys came from and why they had stumbled upon them. Granted, the oceanographers and scientists who were following their strange journey knew their story. Plus, the newscasters covered the story of the container that crashed open, with the contents of toys lost at sea.*

"There were hundreds of beachcombers and residents along the coastal areas of countries, continents, and waterways of the world following this. It must have been a fun mystery of where and why they suddenly appeared from out of nowhere.

"That's the amazement I felt. And it made me feel some of the surprises I felt as I watched those T.V. shows involving weird science."

"Hey, Philip," she said. "I did watch quite a few of those science T.V. shows you were referring to."

"Oh yeah? Prove it!" he laughed.

"Well, did you know that a bowling ball can float?"

"No, they're way too heavy! That's common sense."

"Not necessarily," smiled Grace. "Now, I'll enlighten you with the facts and the science behind which bowling balls will float and why it happens."

"I'm all ears," Philip said sarcastically.

"It's all about density and the official standards of how the bowling balls are made.

Grace let that sink in for a second and then continued, "The floating only works if they have a density of less than 1(g/mL) grams per milliliter, meaning less than 12 pounds. So an 8-pound or 10-pound bowling ball will float. 12 pounds is the magic balance and can go either way. Bowling balls marked 12 lbs have a density very close to 1 g/mL and will sink, hover, or float. Bowling balls greater than 12 lbs will sink. So what do you think of that?"

Philip thought about that for a minute and smiled as he said, "First of all, I think you watched too much T.V... That being said, I'll never be able to bowl again without remembering the fascinating news about the Floating Bowling Balls! That puts you over the top with interesting trivia that I'll never be able to erase out of my head.

"In fact, out of the goodness of my heart and, of course, to show my appreciation for all the thingamabobs in your Survival Kit; (not to mention the ridiculous stuff about Floating Bowling Balls,) ...You may keep this yellow rubber duck! It's come a long way, Baby, and you deserve it."

Chapter 23

Hail! Hail! The gang's all here!

When they landed in Tahiti, Kate obtained an update from, The Coast Guard's HC-130J Super Hercules, which provides long-range surveillance. The FLIR, Forward Looking Infrared Radar camera with extreme zoom, provides them with a great advantage. The aircraft offers heavy air transport and long-range maritime patrol capability in the Pacific Ocean. They had been looking into the missing person case of Grace and Philip.

She was informed that "No, they had not yet been found. Yes, they had a positive visual of the yellow seaplane. However, it was unanchored and afloat with no passengers."

"The only other strange event was a huge flock of birds from the sanctuary that had been struck, and dismembered bird parts were scattered everywhere. The workers at the facility have never seen anything like it."

On the way to the resort, Maggie and Kate called Grace's parents and arranged to meet in the lobby.

Kate will join the United States Coast Guard Search and Rescue team flying the FEACT's Dolphin helicopter. Her transportation is on its way to pick her up. She explained to Grace's parents, "The Coast Guard has already planned out a zig-zag search pattern to carefully spot and outline their location. Then they'll send the appropriate help to rescue Grace and Philip.

"According to what the officers are searching for (a boat, a human, a human with a life jacket, and so forth), they use different search patterns to spot them. That leads to their rescue."

"Oh, I see your car pulling up. I'll see you in a minute," Sarah replied.

As they stepped into the open-air lobby of the Tahiti Hilton Resort, Kate and Maggie immediately rushed to Grace's parents. Sarah asked, "Have you heard anything new about Grace?"

"No, we'll get debriefed soon. Then we'll know more," explained Maggie.

Grace's mom said, "I need to tell you one important thing. The manager here said Joe is furious. He's threatening to sue everybody, including the resort, the manager, and the guy who kidnapped her."

"Don't worry," said Maggie. "I'll step in if Joe goes too far. We need to follow the facts, and I doubt Grace would do anything reckless. I personally think she'd be delighted to go up in that seaplane. After all, she's already a licensed pilot. Completing the seaplane certification is the next thing on her bucket list."

Sarah explained, "The manager told us that Philip was perfectly harmless. It was his little yellow seaplane that might be a problem. It appears that he's always tinkering with it down by the shore."

Maggie had been struggling with this awkward dilemma since she saw the photo of the accused kidnapper. *"How much did the resort really know about him?"*

Chapter 24

That evening, a spectacular sunset was displayed for the adventurous duo on the uninhabited island. The little seaplane was slowly riding the waves back to them. They were making bets with each other as to the time and location that it would arrive. What a wonderful experience! Not a care in the world for these two.

Grace mentioned, "The high tides are uneven. We'll hope that the height for this high tide tonight will be extraordinary and bring the seaplane all the way back to this area. If so, we can guide it back to our campsite. Wouldn't it be wild if we could retie it to the same tree?"

"No," Philip insisted, "We need to drag it more inland, so we don't lose it again. We have to repair the engine and get back to the resort tomorrow. We're not on Springbreak, ya know!"

After a moment, he added, "Hey would you like to learn to catch a fish with your hands? I know you've got lots of neat tools and gadgets from your adventure kit, but I know to fish with your bare hands. It's an invaluable survival skill, allowing you to harvest food with zero equipment. You can take this back to your survival fanatics and show them how to fish like this."

"Okay, okay! This sounds so cool, as well as useful. It better not be some kind of a trick to make me fall headfirst into the water!"

"Why I'm insulted that you'd even suggest it. Now come over here. We'll lean out where this long branch extends over the water. Now slowly put your arm into the water up to your elbow."

"Like this?" asked Grace.

"Yes, keep it very still. It's going to get nice and cool. It might take about ten minutes."

Philip whispered, "When you see a fish, extend your index finger toward it and wiggle it slightly back and forth, imitating a worm, until he sees it."

"That's so funny," said Grace.

"It's called noodling, but no talking until we get our supper," he chuckled.

"When you connect with the fish, and it moves close enough, grab it by the gills and pull it out. Voila!"

After a few minutes, Grace saw a curious fish coming her way. She patiently followed directions and signaled the fish by noodling it. Sure enough, she pulled out a fish, to Grace's amazement. She was so surprised that she screamed, laughed, and flung it, flopping, onto the sand a few feet away. "It's a miracle!" she yelled.

They had great success with their fishing technique during the next half hour, as they landed a few more fish. Grace sheepishly admitted, "I never thought I'd learn how to fish like this. I try to learn something every day, but this wasn't ever on my list. I didn't know anyone could do this! Thank you, Philip!"

"That's quite alright. This was my first time too. I just wanted to see if 'You' could do it," he laughed. "Hey, I'm just kidding!"

As they dried themselves off and walked back toward the fires, Grace asked, "What is the plan for this evening?"

"Well, I think we've kept the fires going in daylight for the smoke and mirror signals. We did great. I'm just thinking about the 1,359 square miles of French Polynesia, scattered over 1,200 miles of ocean. That's a whole lot of islands and atolls to search. We'd better plan on getting ourselves out of this situation."

Grace was eager to brag about the Sea Crest Lighthouse and its local Coast Guard's successes, and she was going to start right now. "Well, Philip, for your information, my best girlfriends are a Coast Guard Search and Rescue helicopter pilot and an FBI Special Agent. In fact, my other best friend partners with me as we volunteer to fly for humanitarian organizations. Aviation Without Borders, Angel Flight, Samaritans Purse, and St Jude's Hospital. Mary Beth and I work together, alternating as a pilot and co-pilot team, to fill in during our free time."

"You're kidding me, right?" Philip was stunned.

"No, I wouldn't kid about the talents of these wonderful women. In fact, Kate is a helicopter pilot; she can fly anything, but she loves her search and rescue job the best. When we were in high school, she was the first to learn to fly. She encouraged Mary Beth and me to get our pilots licenses before graduating high school."

"That's outstanding! Do you think they'll be involved with our delay in returning to the resort?"

Grace thought about that for a minute, then said, "Well, one of my friends, Joe, was supposed to call me. I don't know what he was told when he called the resort yesterday. He didn't even know I was coming to Tahiti. He was in court all day, and I left a message for him."

"Is he in some kind of trouble? Why was he in court?"

Grace laughed, "No, he's an attorney. He never has his phone on when he's in court, so I left him a message."

"Oh, is he your boyfriend or something?"

"Well, that's a good question. We're best friends, and we spend all our free time together and have lots of fun. I found that I really miss not sharing this adventure with him."

Grace quickly regretted that remark and tried to correct her tactlessness. "Oh, No! I didn't mean that you're not great. No offense to you."

"Okay, none taken," Philip laughed. "I'm sure he misses you too."

"I hope so."

After a moment of reflection, she added, "Remember when we talked about your resemblance to Antonio Banderas?"

"Of course."

"Well, I've often thought my attorney friend, Joe, also looks like a movie star."

"Really? Who does he look like?"

"I always thought he looked a little like Pierce Brosnan. Maybe it's more like he acts like him. I'm not exactly sure. However, I've seen others, even complete strangers, also see the likeness."

"What makes you think that?"

"Well, I've only gotten close to Joe over the past year. My first example relates to the fact that we're both huge movie fans. We love to see movies together, even older ones."

"You mean like a date night where you rent a movie?"

"No, we have a diner theater in our area called, The Playhouse. When they don't have a live performance playing, they've started to show movies. They usually feel good, with a great plot and music."

"That sounds very enjoyable."

"It's turned out to be a big success. People come from around the area to attend the special Dinner and Movie nights. It keeps the cash flow coming in between their plays. It also keeps their audience regularly coming to great performances at The Playhouse."

"Okay, it sounds like someone thought Joe resembles someone on the big screen or in a live performance."

Grace laughed, "Well, our live performances are more along the lines of Community Theater or Off, Off (Hoping to make

94

Broadway) entertainment. We don't have known actors in our cast. However, we have several actors who are Screen Actor's Guild members.

"Of course, they have specific rules to follow if they act for non-profits or productions that are not involved with the Screen Actor's Guild.

"Well, did they think Joe resembled Pierce Brosnan?"

"First, remember that many audience members are from out of town and don't know that we are probably just regular people. With that said, a few months ago, we saw *The Thomas Crown Affair.*

"Joe and I had already discovered how much we loved great movies. When we talked about our favorite movies, we both mentioned that movie. When we heard they were showing it at The Playhouse, we ensured we had tickets.

"Well, the waiters, with bowler hats, served apple pie, with a slice of green apple on top, for dessert while changing the reels. A lady stepped over to Joe's seat and asked him for his autograph."

"Wow! That must have been a thrill for him."

"Oh yes! He smiled as he signed *Denis Leary* on her playbill!"

The lady gushed, "Oh, thank you, as she turned to leave, she glanced at the signature and stopped."

"Joe said in a British accent, 'Oh, did you think I'm Pierce Brosnan? No, I'm just a regular fan.' They both laughed as she returned to her seat."

Philip laughed, saying, "Joe sounds like a great guy!"

"He is, for sure. One of our favorite things about that night (aside from the mistaken identity) is that we got to hear '*The Windmills of Your Mind*' with their auditorium's beautiful sound system. It was magnificent," Grace ended wistfully.

After a minute, he continued, "Well, I think we'd better use one of our three fires to cook the fish we caught. I'm good at fixing the supper if it's alright with you."

"Yes, that sounds good. I'll open some extra coconuts and gather extra wood to keep the fires going tonight."

"Plus, we need to keep our eyes on that seaplane," he remarked. He turned and looked over his shoulder and saw the seaplane had now rode a wave into the area nearby and moved almost within reach if they hurried. Philip yelled, "Come On! It's almost here!" as he jumped in the water and waded out to meet it!

Grace joined him, happily bringing the seaplane up to the shore. "What an incredible day we've had!" Grace yelled to Philip as they secured the seaplane to a new tree farther inland.

Later as they ate their fish under the stars, Grace proclaimed, "Isn't this the best?"

"Well, if you're referring to my cooking skills, the night sky with those beautiful constellations, or the fact that we have my seaplane back, then it's the best!" he laughed.

"Now, all we need is to be rescued or get the seaplane fixed," she added.

"Do you think your friends would come here to help search for us?"

"As soon as they know I'm in trouble, they'll come."

"What about the FBI Special Agent? Does she fly too?" he asked cautiously.

"Well, she's involved with a lot of international stuff that she can't talk about. But rest assured, Maggie O'Hara is a force to be reckoned with!"

Philip did a double take as he choked on his fish! *"Wow! Maggie? That's an understatement!"*

Chapter 25

Back at the Hilton Tahiti Resort, they were looking at the same magnificent sunset. The Sea Crest guests were spread out informally, telling each other why they had come to Tahiti. The Search and Rescue plans were really moving along. Kate gathered everyone into an area of the open-air atrium. She started, "The resort has invited us to use this wonderful semi-private area of the atrium as a base for our rescue of Kate and Philip. The alcove area opens into a conservatory room. It's just to the right of the huge expanse overlooking and leading down to the beautiful ocean. The staff will arrange more plants and a beautiful Japanese folding screen with a mural on both sides. This conservatory will keep our privacy, and we'll have comfortable seating and round-the-clock coffee, tea, and various drinks at our disposal. They'll also bring in trays of fruit and Tahiti baked goods. We have a few beautiful carved desks with wifi and laptop computers. This is where we can set up our communication headquarters with the best view in the universe."

Maggie ushered everyone into the area with overstuffed armchairs, sofas, and lounge chaises. It was made for comfort. When everyone was settled, she picked up where Kate had left off. "You may ask why the resort is being so hospitable. The answer lies in the fact that although Grace approached the young man and asked for a ride in his seaplane, the hotel manager gave her the understanding that she would be safe. The manager is also concerned on behalf of this young man, who is extremely likable and hard working. The hotel, therefore, intends to do everything possible to safely find them both. We assume that although Grace wanted to get a look at French Polynesia from the air, she also wanted to see the Venus Pointe Lighthouse. The location where we'll start the search tomorrow is on the way to the lighthouse. That's where the seaplane was floating when we had last visual contact."

The manager entered the alcove and explained, "We are so sorry that their return was delayed. We have no reason to believe that Ms. Cook was harmed in any way by the young man. Philip is a quiet man employed by our resort for about one year. He appears to spend most of his free time tinkering with his seaplane. He keeps mostly to himself though he's very observant. Kind of a people watcher, if you will."

"Ms. Cook inquired if her French was good enough to have him understand that she wanted to come back here because he spoke no English. I did explain to her that Philip was fine but that none of us would go up in that ... *'I better not say, that bucket of bolts.'* ... Let's just say those of us that work here are not ... *'used to taking risks. No, better not say that'... eager to 'die?'* "Let's just say that we've never asked Philip if we could ride in his seaplane."

"Well," he finished, "We want to do everything within our power to help find our Philip and Ms. Cook."

"Thank you for everything you're doing," said Grace's father quietly.

Kate stepped up and verified the plans she had made with the International Water Safety Association. "Well, first thing in the morning, I'll fly the United States Coast Guard Dolphin helicopter to the coordinates where they spotted the little yellow seaplane. Even if it's no longer visible, we'll closely search the vicinity for any sign of Grace and Philip."

She did not mention what they all feared, *"Why they were not in the seaplane is very disturbing, but there could be a reasonable explanation. I just have to go to that location and see if there is anything that will lead to their rescue. I'll start there tomorrow morning. Hopefully, they are both alive and well."*

The group from Sea Crest compared notes on why they were each there. It became evident that Grace wanted to share the possible connection to Captain James Cook with her parents. Her Mom had brought the orphan Key to try in the locket to prove that he was related to them. Of course, that all depended on them finding the cornerstone from the original Venus Pointe Lighthouse, which was repaired in 1965.

Attorney Jeffery Williams was busy looking over documentation from the files on Captain James Cook and the repair of the Venus Pointe Lighthouse. He shared, "It doesn't mention that the cornerstone was found in 1965, but it discusses the various materials displayed at the lighthouse museum. It appears that there is another different location for Captain James Cook's information. I'll have to check each one for possible cornerstone artifacts. Let's see the Museum of Tahiti and the Islands and the information at the Venus Pointe Lighthouse."

Mary Beth explained to Grace's parents, " I drove Grace to the airport. I was so excited that she was going to Tahiti. I reminisced about my trip to France after high school with my sister. The more I talked, the more I longed to revisit France. By the time I returned home, I had decided to share the French Polynesia adventure with Grace. So I packed my bags and took the next flight."

"Well, we're glad you're here," said Grace's mom, Sarah. "I have every hope that Grace will be found tomorrow."

"By the way," Mary Beth continued. "I know Grace would have loved to go up in that seaplane. However, I am disheartened to learn that this 'repairman' took her for a ride." Mary Beth silently continued to degrade this guy, *"I truly hope he gets everything that he deserves if he harmed one hair on her head! Of course, Grace is so naive and trusting that she wouldn't expect anyone would hurt her! The more I think about this guy, the more I hate him."*

Sarah was also very concerned for her daughter's safety, *"However, I don't want to think the worst. I want to remain positive and believe they'll find her."*

James Cook looked around the atrium and was grateful for all these friends who had assembled to help his daughter. *"It appears that each person is here to support their daughter, Grace."*

However, they had no idea of the serious events about to unfold upon their arrival.

Chapter 26

Meanwhile, back in Sea Crest, Joe again drank multiple cups of coffee. He quickly repacked his suitcases and reviewed yesterday's debacle: *"I'm not dragging those stupid tools into the airport today!!! How could I be that dumb? Well, I had a lot on my mind. Good Grief, I hope Grace is okay. I'll call the resort and check on that right now."*

He stepped over to the desk and dialed the number. A young lady answered the phone, "Hello, The Tahiti Hilton. How may I help you?"

"Hello. I'd like to speak with Grace Cook or be transferred to her room."

"I'm sorry, Sir. She isn't here at the moment. I can put you through to her room, and you can leave a message if you'd like!"

Joe did not like this at all. "No problem, However, I need to talk to the manager right now!"

"Oh, … well, I can have him call you back…."

"I'll wait!"

"I'll have to go track him down…."

"Yes, that's a good idea. And tell him I'm Joe Lawrence. I spoke with him yesterday. I should say, I warned him yesterday that Grace had better be there, Safe and Sound, when I arrived at the Tahiti Hilton Hotel."

"Oh, you're coming here?" she said nervously.

"Yes, you can count on it. Now would you please get your manager on the phone?"

"He's talking with a group of people, but I'll try to get his attention."

"Yes, I'd say that's a great idea." Joe was getting more frustrated by the minute. He was scared that he might never see Grace again. He regretted all the lost opportunities to tell her how much he loved her.

After, what felt like a lifetime, the manager picked up the receiver and said, "Hello, how may I help you!"

"Hello, This is Joe Lawrence. I'd like to know where Grace Cook is!"

"Sir, we have the United States Coast Guard Search and Rescue Team. They are working with the International South Pacific coastguard network in this missing person search. They are setting up the plan and have every hope of finding them today."

"Oh, did Kate Jensen and Maggie Jensen arrive? Great! I am confident they will be able to find our kidnapped victim, Grace. I have no interest in the other fugitive from justice except to see that he gets what he deserves. I will also hold you personally responsible and your resort."

"We are doing everything possible to find them."

"You can save that boloney for the International Bureau of Investigation!" Joe said as he slammed down the receiver.

Chapter 27

Grace and Philip sat by the fires and listened to the sound of the surf as it rolled in. "Look at all these stars," marveled Philip.

"Yes, it's pretty impressive."

Philip said, "Can I ask you something, Grace?"

"Sure, ask away!"

"When you told me that you were a historian and something about a note from Robert Louis Stevenson. I have a question about authors in general."

"Okay, tell me what you'd like to know, and I'll tell you what I know or think about them. Sometimes we don't know the whole truth about famous people. That being said, what is your question?"

"Well, I'm very interested in people and their lives. The Tahiti Hilton has guests from all over the world. One day I watched a couple of ladies play a card game named Authors."

"Yes, I'm familiar with that game. In fact, I used to play it myself. So what's your question?"

"Well, the authors are probably from a previous time, like your author, Robert Louis Stevenson. I think he wrote Treasure Island. Right?"

Grace nodded, yes.

"Now, my favorite author was probably Mark Twain. I liked to read Tom Sawyer and Huckleberry Finn. Have you read either of them?"

"Yes, I've read and enjoyed both books," Grace answered.

"Well, my interest is that they were in the set of a card game named Authors. I overheard these two ladies talking at length about these real authors, and I wondered if the authors actually met each other. Did they like the writing of the other author? Did they have the same problems? Were they rich or poor while writing their books, or did they become popular after they died?"

"I love that you are interested in those parts of their lives. I know a little about Robert Louis Stevenson's and Mark Twain's lives, so I can share what I've learned."

"That would be great," remarked Philip.

"Mark Twain is the pen name of American author Samuel Clemens. He was a riverboat captain and loved his job on the Mississippi River. The paddleboats had to travel at least two fathoms or 12 feet deep on the water. 'Mark Twain' was the leadman's call when the boat was in safe water.

"Mark Twain was how Samuel Clemens signed his first article in 1893 as a newspaper reporter in Nevada. He continued to use it throughout his life.

"He was not only a contemporary of Robert Louis Stevenson, but they also enjoyed each other's company and writing. Many think Stevenson's, Treasure Island, was based on Tom Sawyer. According to Professor Hubbard, who taught a course on the similarities between the two authors, Stevenson stated that he wanted to meet Huckleberry Finn's grandfather.

"The two men used to meet on a bench in Washington Square in NYC and chat for hours. They had a mutual admiration society thing going on.

"One thing they had in common was their poor childhood illnesses, caregivers, and childhood fantasies growing up.

"Stevenson was born November 13, 1850, in Edinburgh, Scotland. He was a sickly child and suffered chronic lung ailments that confined him to his bed for much of his childhood. The respiratory symptoms typical of tuberculosis included breathing difficulties and spitting up blood.

"He spent a lot of time thinking about his own mortality.

"His beloved nurse, Crummy, cared for him and told him stories about pirates, great sailing ships, and buried treasure. He dedicated the book, *A Child's Garden of Verses,* to his dear friend.

"His poor health persisted throughout his life with coughing, fevers, lung problems, and great weakness. He spent the winter of 1887 at Saranac Lake under the care of Dr. E.L. Trudeau at what he called The Adirondack Cottages for Treatment of Pulmonary Disease. They named the cottage where he stayed, The Robert Louis Stevenson Cottage (formerly Baker Cottage.)

"There was also a time when Robert Louis Stevenson traveled from Europe to New York City. He planned to continue by train across the United States to the West Coast. However, his health was feeble when he arrived in New York. So he accepted an invitation to stay at Mr. Fairchild's estate in New Port, Rhode Island, to rest and recuperate. During his stay, he heard about Ida Lewis. She was the female lightkeeper stationed to oversee the Lime Rock lighthouse off the coast of Rhode Island. He was amazed at her many heroic rescues of people drowning in the Atlantic Ocean.

"Her father was the original lightkeeper, but he suffered a stroke and became disabled after only four months. The workload of his job was passed down to the fifteen-year-old Ida.

"Ida expanded her domestic duties to caring for her invalid father, her seriously ill sister, and her regular lighthouse duties.

"The Lime Rock lighthouse was surrounded by water. One of Ida's unique talents was rowing a huge wooden boat across the ocean waters to get supplies and equipment for the family. She saved many lives, using her famous boat to get them to safety.

"She was also known as the best swimmer in Newport. In 1881, she was awarded a rare Gold Lifesaving Medal by the United States government. It was the first ever given to a woman.

"Ida's proud father enjoyed counting the number of people who came to the island to see his famous daughter. This time in lighthouse history was full of numerous heroes. I love reading about them."

Philip replied, "Thank you for sharing all that historical knowledge. It's all new to me ."

"You're certainly welcome," Grace answered. "Now, let's turn to Samuel Clemens, born on November 30, 1835, two months premature. He continued in relatively poor health for the first 10 years. During this time, death from fever and disease was not unusual. In his family, four of his six brothers and sisters died before age twenty.

"His mother tried various alternative-medicine remedies, including bloodletting, the spirit of caster, and an assortment of water treatments on him during these years. The goal to achieve the healing effects of medicine often proved ineffective. These practices were desperate attempts to save her children's lives during a time when medical vaccines and proven, successful medication had not been discovered yet. Clemens' memories of these instances of his growing up can be found woven into *The Adventures of Tom Sawyer* and various other writings.

"That reminds me of a true story about a 200-page, 1859-era medical book used during the Civil War. With much success, the book contained homemade remedies used for centuries by European ancestors and Native Americans alike. Along with medicinal flowers, they used home-grown plants and herbs and native-found plants growing wild in the area. They'd pound them into salves and ointments or make them into herbal teas.

"Many people in those times that also lived along the rivers died because they didn't have access to quinine medicine. The cost for quinine was as high as $560. The book told of making their own quinine from Magnolia tree bark. This could protect your family from malaria.

Philip added, "I've heard that some of these same plants play a big part in the current drugs. However, the costs are high, to say the least.

"Because the death of four of her children had been such a cruel reality, Clemens' mother often fussed over and pampered him. This led to his early tendency to get attention from her through mischief. He developed a sense of justice for his petty crimes and shared his mother's good nature and sense of humor.

"When his mother was in her 80's, they still shared their delightful repartee. Clemens was overheard asking her about his poor health in those early years: "I suppose that during that whole time, you were uneasy about me?" "Yes, the whole time," she answered. "Afraid I wouldn't live?" "No," she said, "afraid you would."

"Clemens's interests as a young lad growing up were playing at being pirates, Robin Hood, and rafting adventures along the river. One close friend was Tom Blankenship, a pleasant but impoverished boy whom Twain said was who he based his character of Huckleberry Finn.

"Mark Twain greatly loved cats and preferred them to humans. That might not be evident after reading the cat and the pain killer scene in *The Adventures of Tom Sawyer*. At one time, he had up to 19 cats.

"Mark Twain also stayed at Saranac Lake for a summer and enjoyed the canoes that traveled past his cottage. It's said that Saranac Lake managed to attract its share of famous visitors. In journalism, no greater names existed than Robert Louis Stevenson and Mark Twain. Very little was recorded on Twain's visit. However, the cottage where he vacationed is known locally as the Mark Twain Camp."

Grace finished by saying, "Yes, there were a lot of similarities in their lives."

"Thanks, that was great listening to your information about them."

"When we get back to the resort, if you think of any other authors you're curious about, I may have some interesting thoughts on their lives."

Philip reminded her that they'd better get some sleep. "I think we'll be spotted tomorrow. By the way, when other people are around, could you do me a favor?"

"Of course, anything!" Grace laughed.

"This is very important…Well, I don't want to lose my job. I'm going to lay low for a while. If you do see me, could we please…only speak French? Nobody knows I can speak English."

Chapter 28

"What am I missing?" Philip closed his eyes, but he didn't fall asleep right away. *"If Grace is on the level and isn't planning a drug drop at the Venus Pointe Lighthouse, how can I make the deal? I was sure she was my contact when I saw her come toward my seaplane with that crazy French language nonsense about going up in my seaplane.*

"I've seen every possible trick in the book, but she takes the cake. This place has been like Grand Central Station with all the drug action in the last 10 days. In the lobby, I saw the headlines for the Journaux de la Polynésie Française newspaper. 'Two seizures in Tahiti collected one and a half metric tons (3,300 pounds) of the drug while they were in transit to Australia.' When I quickly scanned the news article, they mentioned something else that related to me. 'Last week, two sailboats were intercepted by the French army in French Polynesia after a tip by the French secret services. French Polynesia is a huge French maritime territory in the South Pacific, spanning the area of Europe. A lot of space for traffickers to pass incognito, but not this time: 1,438 kilograms (3,236 pounds) of cocaine were found in the operation, and three suspects were arrested and transported to mainland France. A fourth suspect is armed and dangerous and on the loose.' APS

"Well, they didn't suspect me...yet! If we are rescued tomorrow, there will be a lot of publicity coverage for the story.

My life will be in danger from the drug cartel bosses. They've got Fentanyl coming in, and I'm nowhere to be found."

Chapter 29

Meanwhile, sleep did not come easily for Grace either. She was carefully rethinking the question of whether Joe was her boyfriend. *"Over the past year, I've grown much closer to him. It's not as though I had anyone else interested in me, but there is no one else I'd rather be with."*

"Okay, the moment of truth! Does Joe want to be romantically involved with me, or am I just a convenient best friend?

"If we did want to date, would we lose our special friendship?

"What if we talk about it and Joe decides to keep us as friends while he wants to date someone else?...... Well, that would devastate me," she realized with a jolt.

"Why hasn't he ever really asked me out on a 'date'? Granted, he always asks me to be his 'partner in crime.' We were both having the time of our lives, setting up Maggie and James.

Grace's thoughts were going down a path that was causing her great sorrow. *"Maybe he'd still like to do things like that but still not want to fall in love with me. Maybe I'm not his type. The type that he's attracted to.*

"Alright, who have I seen him date? Granted, until this last year, I wouldn't have even noticed. Okay, I never noticed, but we

have an influx of tourists here during the summer. Some of them are interesting, talented, and very nice looking. As a matter of fact, I think people, in general, try to get in perfect shape before going on vacation every year. They want to look their best in their swimsuits. They always show up here with their manicure, pedicure, and hair looking their best.

Grace thought of how she must look. *"Yes, I look like a ship-wrecked female historian with the worst-looking hands, feet, and hair possible. The only level I could compete on was my survival skills and my suntan.*

She almost laughed as she dejectedly thought, *"Well, if Joe is attracted to the look of a hurricane survivor's worse day, then I've got a shot!*

"Well, I do believe we'll get rescued tomorrow. That will mean I'll see Joe next week after discovering if my family is related to Robert Louis Stevenson. That will be the longest time that we've been apart since we started hanging out together. In fact, this couple of days is already the longest time apart."

Grace felt terrible as she shut her tearful eyes and tried to get to sleep. Her problem was not that she wasn't sleepy. It was that she had just realized that she was in love with Joe Lawrence.

Chapter 30

At daybreak the following day, as the pilot in command, Kate climbed into the front seat of the US Coast Guard Dolphin Helicopter. She also had access to the Coast Guard Hercules aircraft, if needed. This international team of Search and Rescue professionals was the best in the world. Kate checked through the pre-flight tests and filed their flight plan. They were going to meet the Coast Guard ship at the coordinates where they had seen the yellow seaplane floating yesterday.

The tower cleared Kate for takeoff, and the SARS team headed towards yesterday's sighting of the yellow seaplane. It was disturbing that the little seaplane had been empty. However, that was where they were starting this morning.

Meanwhile, Grace and Philip were gathering wood for a few smoke signals. Grace called out an optimistic prediction, "I think today will be a terrific day! I just know we'll be rescued."

"Well, I sure hope you're right. I see our seaplane is still where we left it, but I'm not sure I can fix the engine. I don't have spare parts in my toolbox."

"You're probably right. I guess we better make super-effective smoke signals. I need a little extra energy to do that," she laughed. "I'm going to use a new coconut bowl to pick a large supply of those delicious coffee beans. You make the best coffee, Philip."

"Oh, it's my pleasure. Do you want yours with vanilla beans or coconut?"

"I'd like both and keep them coming. How often will we be able to drink your special 'campfire' coffee?"

"I'm not sure. However, we need to wet these palms' branches and soak the jacket to make the most of our smoke signals," Philip reminded her.

"Let's realign the letters of our messages on the beach," she said. "We need to have the best visibility possible."

"Yes, don't forget the signal mirror."

The smoke signals perfectly displayed puffs of white smoke drifting upwards from the three fires. They sat down to rest and enjoy their coffee and version of trail mix; (pineapple chunks, coconut pieces, and berries).

"Do you think we should move the yellow seaplane out in the open?" asked Grace.

"Well, it can't hurt. It's big enough to draw attention and help identify us."

They untied the little yellow seaplane, and with one on each side, they tugged it to and fro until it slid across the sand to an open spot.

"Hey," said Philip. "How would you like to build a sandcastle while we're waiting to get rescued?"

"Wow," Grace laughed. "You know, That's a splendid idea! I haven't made one since I was a child."

"Well, I think it's fun," explained Philip. "I made a lighthouse sandcastle for a contest once. We can dig a hole near the seaplane and fill it with water. Then the fun begins when we start to pack the giant mound of wet sand. I think this sand is a perfect consistency for building a compact base.

"Of course, making a sandcastle of The Venus Pointe Lighthouse would be fun. The picturesque white Victorian-Era lighthouse is the only lighthouse in Tahiti. It reminds me of a square-shaped, six-layer wedding cake. It will be easy to make because of its shape."

"Yes, I love the look of The Venus Pointe Lighthouse also. I'll collect the coconut cups to use as scoops, and we can use things from your toolbox and my survival kit to work with. I had difficulty sleeping last night, and I hope we get rescued today. However, this is a great way to spend the day today."

"Thanks for being such a good sport about everything. I don't know how things will go after we get rescued. Still, this project is an enjoyable opportunity to relax before all the chaos."

After a while, the sand pile looked like the famous lighthouse. With Grace's Swiss Army Knife and Philip's triangle ruler and scraper, it was coming together very nicely.

"Wow, Philip, you're really talented a this," exclaimed Grace as she sat back and looked at the beautiful sand sculpture."

"Thanks! I was always fascinated by sandcastles and the artists that created them. I don't take the time to make them myself too often." What he meant was, *"I don't want to draw attention to myself."*

Grace wished she could take a few pictures of the beautiful sandcastle! She was almost sad as she reflected, *"This is the end of a dream come true. I don't ever want to forget this fun day. Will anything ever top this? Yet, why does it feel like a hollow victory? It makes me think of the song by Peggy Lee. 'Is this all there is? If it's all there is, then let's keep ... What?"*

"This over-shadowing feeling seems to be constantly returning to me. Are my feeling of love one-sided?"

It was like a melancholy reminder that the part that completed her was absent. *"I never dreamed how big and important Joe has become to me. I don't know when I've had such a magnificent opportunity to enjoy such a meaningful journey. I can't truly feel it completely because I miss Joe. It's like an important piece of my heart is actually mourning the loss of him."*

Then a happy thought occurred to her. *"What am I so worried about? I'll be seeing him in a few days."* That's when reality hit her.

"What if he doesn't feel the same love for me?"

Chapter 31

Kate's, Search and Rescue Mission was not having any luck locating the spot where the seaplane had been seen yesterday. She put the orders in to call NOAA's physical oceanographers working in this area. They study the physical conditions and physical processes within the ocean, such as waves, currents, eddies, gyres, and tides;

A short time later, NOAA responded with an answer of where the yellow craft would be today. The helicopter set its search to an uninhabited island several miles away. Kate called a message into the Coast Guard Cutter in that vicinity. "We have new coordinates for the two missing persons."

The Captain of the Coast Guard Cutter responded immediately, "Great! We saw smoke signals coming from a small island. We are headed there now. We also just picked up a mirror signal from the same island. This is great! If it's who we're searching for, they are alive and able to build fires and send signals. Wonderful!"

The SARS Helicopter and Coast Guard Cutter soon reached the island. Grace and Philip happily waved the huge palm branches in the air with sheer happiness. "I knew they would come today!" Grace shouted as the blades of the helicopter swooshed overhead.

Kate lowered the helicopter to the beach, and with great joy, she turned off the engine, unhooked her seatbelt, took off her helmet, and climbed down to the sand. Grace greeted her with open arms, "Boy, are we glad to see you!"

Kate passionately shouted, "The yellow seaplane was spotted yesterday, and no one was on it. We were so afraid that we had lost you. Are you both okay? "

"Yes," stated Philip and Grace together.

"What an adventure we had," declared Grace. "Boy, was my survival kit a great help! I learned so much about how to actually fly and repair the seaplane. We flew over a bird sanctuary, and the birds got caught in our engine. Philip made a super landing on this beach, and we've been having a wonderful time. I knew you'd come, Kate!"

"Wow, look at this sandcastle!" Kate exclaimed. "It looks just like the Venus Pointe Lighthouse! It's beautiful. How did you guys do this?"

"It was Philip's idea. He's won an award for another one he made." Grace continued with great pride, "I helped. I learned how to make them solid so you can work on the details without them falling apart. It's so much fun!"

"Well, I radioed that we found you, Grace," said Kate. "The United States Coast Guard Cutter just offshore is waiting to take you onboard for medical treatment."

"Oh, my folks were going to come to Tahiti. I'm not sure when they'll arrive, but I don't want them to worry."

"Grace, they've already arrived, and Yes, they were plenty worried. However, I called to report that I spotted you. You were happily waving your arms and palm leaves in the air. They know you're safe."

"Oh no, I didn't even think anyone would know about this except you. I knew you'd rescue us."

Next, Kate turned to Philip and quietly said, "Let's walk. How are you feeling? Did you want to go to the Coast Guard Cutter and get medical help?"

"No, I'm feeling just fine. I have to talk with the authorities about a couple of things. Maybe you can help me with that."

"Yes, I know someone on the Coast Guard Cutter would like to meet with you. I'll drop you off on their deck. Does Grace need to be debriefed about anything?"

Grace was gathering coconuts far enough away from them that she couldn't hear anything they were saying.

"No, she knows nothing except that I'm a handyman with a seaplane. We only conversed in French until the bird strike on the engine. I told her we must go back to speaking French when we return to Tahiti. "

Kate nodded and said, "I know nothing about who you are, but I've got a good idea of what you're involved in. For your safety, we may have to file a report that you didn't survive. We must get Grace onboard with that story before we return to Tahiti."

"Can Grace and I go to the Coast Guard Cutter under the ploy of a good meal? That would allow me to take care of my business and make some decisions."

Kate agreed. "Okay, Grace, gather your things; we're stopping off at the Coast Guard Cutter for a good meal before we fly back to Tahiti."

They took pictures with Kate's fully charged phone of the beautiful camp with the three fires, the sand castle lighthouse, the coconuts, the wrecked engine on the front of the seaplane, the bamboo and palm bed shelter, and Grace's prize rubber duck. While clicking through the pictures, she saw the pug pictures of Snarfy.

"Hey, who is the cute pug?" asked Grace.

"You won't believe it, but Michael got me a surprise puppy," answered Kate. "I'll tell you all about him later. However, James and Michael took Misha and Snarfy to the dog park together. Those dogs love each other. James laughed so much, walking the odd couple down the road. The park is separated by the big and little dogs, but there were only a few dogs there today.

Snarfy made a friend with another pug named Louie. It was a riot to watch. They had so much fun, Michael said."

"Louie and Snarfy have a play date Saturday. Can you believe it?"

Grace laughed as she looked around. They had lots of room in the helicopter, so they loaded a few extra coconuts to take back to the resort.

Grace picked up her survival kit and purposely left his tool kit with the little yellow seaplane with the broken engine. Philip also left his soaked jacket that helped make the terrific smoke signals.

As the helicopter took off, Grace had a strange melancholy feeling of loss. *"I guess I'll never get to have a great adventure like this again in my lifetime. I wish I could have had it with Joe. I feel like I will have a different relationship with him now that I'm falling in love with him. What will I do if Joe doesn't feel the same towards me? I don't know if I'll be able to take it. This scares me, and nothing scares me!*

Chapter 32

Kate landed the helicopter on the deck of the United States Coast Guard Cutter. As they exited the aircraft, Maggie stepped into view. She tearfully hugged Grace with relief and said, "We saw that little yellow seaplane adrift in the ocean, and it was empty. We were so scared!"

Next, as Maggie turned to Philip, she tearfully put her hand on his cheek and searched his eyes as she almost whispered, "Are you okay? I thought we'd lost you."

Philip put his arm around her and said, "Oh, Maggie, you know me! I'm like a cat with nine lives!"

"Well, I'm glad you're okay," Maggie laughed. "Now we just have to figure out what we're going to do with you!"

Grace and Kate just stared at them, speechless.

Maggie turned to them and said, "This is the best International Drug Enforcement Special Agent we've ever had. I've requested his help with setting up my new FBI team that I'm putting together at Sea Crest. He had to finish this undercover case on the drugs in the Pacific.

"With Fentanyl, the Duragesic drug from China, flooding into Mexico and on to the United States, we must get it stopped as soon as possible. We have also used sweeping efforts to stop the flow of cocaine and other drugs from the Southern and Central

Americas from reaching The United States' shores. In some cases, the smugglers are captured and brought onto the Coast Guard cutters and shackled to the deck. They are then transported back to the United States for trial."

Philip added, "This created a secret U.S. detention system in the War on Drugs, which involves U.S. Coast Guard cutters sailing in the Pacific Ocean."

They moved inside to the Officers Mess Hall on the US Coast Guard Cutter and sat down. The stewards started serving platers of delicious food and asked for any requests our survivors wanted. "We have an Italian chef who makes some of the best Chicken Parmesan, Stuffed Eggplant, and Pizza specialties you've ever tasted," the steward suggested.

"He's also come up with some dishes based on local food. One of our favorites is called Crunch Topped Oriental Chicken. I think he created it one day, and we loved it."

Philip immediately piped up with a laugh, "Well, this has nothing to do with being stranded on an uninhabited island. However, I'd love a good old American cheeseburger and fries."

"Yes, that sounds great. Make that two! Of course, we ate well, with Philip teaching me how to catch fish by hand. They were deliciously roasted over a campfire, even without my favorite tartar sauce."

"Don't forget our great Vanilla Coconut Lattes and pineapple/berry/coconut trail mix," Philip said proudly. "No worries. We had plenty of good food to eat!"

The stewards quickly returned with the special orders, and everyone started eating.

Between bites, Philip explained, "No one here at the Tahiti Hilton Resort suspects that I have contacts with members of the international law enforcement agencies. As Maggie and I know from working on several international missions, cooperation with foreign law enforcement agencies is essential to the DEA mission.

The trafficking syndicates responsible for the drug trade inside the United States do not operate solely within its borders.

"These cooperations originated around 1949 under the Federal Bureau of Narcotics, one of the DEA's predecessor agencies. At that time, a couple of agents were sent to Turkey, the world's main producer of morphine base. Next, it was sent to France, where the morphine base was converted into heroin and shipped to the United States. With the need for additional agents, international cases gradually increased. By the 1960s and 1970s, federal drug law enforcement agents were conducting major international operations. International efforts at that time focused on reducing marijuana trafficking along the border with Mexico and curbing heroin trafficking by members of the French underworld. This case became known as the 'French Connection.'

"Opium is derived from the bright red poppy flower, grown in Iran and Turkey. The poppy seeds are distilled by a simple process into morphine base, then refined into pure heroin. The final product is diluted for the retail market in the United States. The opium poppy seeds produce morphine, heroin, and other opiates. These plants can be traced back to the earliest of human civilizations. History reflects that this narcotic drug has been used for centuries as both medicine and a drug.

"During the sixth or seventh centuries, opium was introduced in East Asia and China when trade was carried out along the Silk Route. This road connected Europe to India, China, and Central Asia.

"Heroin arrives in the United States by two general and separate routes: The first is from Southeast Asia across the Pacific, which is what my mission is concerned with. The second is from the Middle East through Western Europe. That is what my job covered while I was in France."

"Now that brings us to the current problem. The sad fact that China is supplying so much fentanyl," Maggie added. "Tahiti is a convenient halfway connection to Mexico and the United States."

Grace sympathized as she agreed, "The deaths from even touching fentanyl are off the charts. I hope you can find an answer to stop those illegal drugs from killing more people."

They finished their meal and were having Pineapple Angel Food Cake and Chocolate Mousse for dessert when Kate brought up the issue on everyone's mind. "Well, now we must decide how to handle their rescue."

Philip made the comment that verified everyone's fear, "If I'm believed to have survived my seaplane crash, and they find me, I'll be dead within 24 hours. The authorities and the Cartel have been looking for the third man involved with the huge drug heist. My undercover information on this case will expose me if it reaches the wrong people."

Maggie agreed, "Yes, I believe the only way to keep you safe is to declare that after the bird strike to the engine of your seaplane, you ended up on the deserted island with Grace. However, since Grace looks and acts wonderful, the story will be she survived the sightseeing ride by smoke signals and mirror signals."

"That's a logical solution to our single survival story," said Kate. "They were both able to get to an uninhabited island. Philip refused to aid Grace in getting help, and he left before dawn to float away in the seaplane, hoping to escape justice. We all know the waves were fifteen to twenty feet high during that time. A rouge wave must have swept him overboard. We found his wrecked seaplane in pieces on a shallow atoll over a hundred miles away. The small land mass would have been underwater during high tide. There was no sign of Philip."

"Well, that sounds plausible enough, stated Maggie. The Coast Guard can manage to get the yellow seaplane to an appropriate atoll and leave it there to corroborate our record."

Philip asked, "What's next for me?"

"I'm hoping you can resurface halfway around the world in a little town called Sea Crest and start helping me set up a First-Class FBI lookout along our coastal area," smiled Maggie.

"I was hoping you'd say that," Philip laughed. "Does that mean a whole new identity? I've got my new name all picked out. It's 'Antonio!' and I only speak French!"

"Boy, you came up with that fast!" said Maggie.

Grace laughed, "What are you up to, Philip?"

"You said you have a friend named Mary Beth, who I'd love to meet. Let's see, she has a mad crush on Antonio Banderas, has been to France, and speaks French. I've been told I resemble Antonio. I've also been to France, and I speak fluent French. I'd love to meet her."

"Oh, you'll meet her alright," smiled Kate. "She's the best Realtor in the Sea Crest community. You'll deal with her when you find housing in the area."

"Good! I look forward to seeing her try to sell me a house speaking only French! Let's see if she knows the value of French Francs, Euros, and United States Dollars."

Maggie said, "Before you get too carried away, how would you like to cross off one of your longtime wishes on that endless bucket list of yours?"

Philip responded, "You know me too well. Of course, I'd love to. Which dream adventure did you have in mind? Remember, you've got to develop something special to top the uninhabited island's survival. That achievement is hard to beat!"

Maggie smiled knowingly, "A couple of years ago, I recall your utter excitement after speaking with several cadets from the Coast Guard Academy about the U.S. Coast Guard Tall Ship, 'Eagle.' Does that memory ring a bell with you?"

"Of course," Philip laughed. "I was astounded at the fantastic opportunity that they'd been given."

"Well," Maggie continued. "The Academy conducts a Sailing Tall Ship 'Semester-at-sea' training school for all cadets. To graduate from the Coast Guard Academy, every single cadet must spend at least six weeks aboard the Eagle. The Eagle has 6 miles of rigging and more than 22,000 square feet of sails."

"Last week, they called to find a few good agents, with the proper security clearance, to help with the training for 10-12 day assignments. If you'd like to take advantage of this opportunity, the Captain of this cutter would be happy to set it up for you and provide transportation."

"Wow, You bet! Thanks, Maggie!"

She answered, "You're welcome. That will keep you completely hidden for at least 10 days, giving me time to get back to Sea Crest and fast forward the preparations for you."

Chapter 33

Once again, Joe picked up his luggage, drove to the airport, and cruised the parking lot for an empty space. He could feel his frustration building as the time slipped by. Finally, he saw his chance. He saw a lady coming down the row of cars toward him. He waited for her to back out, and finally, he parked his car. As he got out of his car, a quick glance at his watch proved he was cutting it close.

His arrival at the ATF conveyer belt went smoothly this time. The same two agents recognized him and watched as he successfully made it through without a hitch. One of them said, "Sorry you missed your flight yesterday."

He thought he better quit while he was ahead, so he smiled and added, "Thanks!"

He'd better try to keep out of trouble, *"There, that should put out some good karma."*

When he approached the gate for his flight to Tahiti, the flight was already boarding. He was the last one to hand over his ticket and boarding pass.

The airline agent held out her hand as she asked, "May I see your passport, sir?"

Joe's stared blankly as he practically shouted, "What? Passport? I don't have one. I fly all the time."

"Well, sir, this is an international flight requiring a passport."

"No, you don't understand! I must get to Tahiti as soon as possible. This is an emergency! A loved one has been kidnaped, and she's missing"

Chapter 34

Maggie called James Cook. He was spreading the news at the Resort among their friends that Grace was safe.

Sarah was so relieved. She hugged her husband and thanked God for the miracle. "I'm not sure what condition she'll be in when we see her, but I'm hoping for the best."

James was also apprehensive. "Maggie didn't give me any details except that the United States Coast Guard was on the scene. They will be available to provide medical help and give them food and drinks as needed."

"Yes, we don't have any idea how long it's been since they have eaten."

Mary Beth ran over to them and hugged them both. "I'm so happy," she cried in relief.

Jeffrey Williams asked, "What do you think their condition is?"

James Cook replied, "We don't know any details. However, Grace is alive, and that's all we know now!"

No one seemed to care about the seaplane's pilot except the Tahiti Hilton manager. He was plenty concerned about the likable young man, Philip. The hotel's liability in this emergency was also a major concern.

Chapter 35

At the airport, Joe was shocked that he hadn't even considered a passport. *"Boy, I'm really losing it,"* he thought. *"Of course, I need one to fly to Tahiti."*

The airline agent tried to help, "Sir, do you have an expired passport? Did you ever have a passport?"

Joe shook his head, "No."

"Well, it usually takes several days to get a passport; however, we have a new expedited passport office here at this airport. They just opened up, claiming that if you can get your forms in order, they can have your passport processed today and get documents in as little as 24 hours. This is a brand new location. They claim they can offer an innovative, streamlined passport processing service, including courier services. They can help you complete your documentation and processing here at the airport."

"Where is their office?" Joe asked.

She directed him to their offices and finished by stating, "Wait! You'll need to show one copy of the Proof of Departure. I'll exchange your ticket for the flight you missed today and issue a new ticket for tomorrow's departure of the same flight. They'll copy this and return your new ticket to you."

130

15 minutes later, he stood outside the door of their passport business. It looked like they were ready to close for the night, so Joe hurried in and asked for help. "Hello, I was just denied boarding for a flight to Tahiti because I don't have a US Passport. The airline explained that you offer expedited services in 24 hours. The airline exchanged my original ticket for the same flight tomorrow. This is my Proof of Departure, which you may copy."

"Yes," answered the passport agent. "The 24-hour turn-around time is dependent on completing and submitting this list of these documents, in an error-free condition, with all the various payments in the correct form of payment needed, in the fastest way possible. Our professionals are trained to be highly effective and efficient in all areas of issuing passports and Visas. Our premier courier system gets all the necessary parts of the application sent and received with great haste. The cost is significantly higher than the regular paths to obtain a passport through normal channels."

"Well, I'd appreciate your help in guiding me through the process of your expedited service. What do you need?"

"Step back to the second office and have a seat."

On his way back to the second office, Joe noticed that other people were getting passports and visas this evening. When he sat at the table in his assigned office, three agents came in with laptops to process different needed parts of the application. They asked for his date of birth and city of birth. They magically pulled a copy of his birth certificate and generated a copy.

A photographer came in and took a headshot of him. She showed him the photo and asked Joe, "Do you like the picture?"

Surprised, he said, "I guess it's okay."

"You're welcome to use the men's room and comb your hair if you'd like. These pictures will represent you for the next ten years. We'd like you to be happy with them."

Joe excused himself and went to the men's room. He looked in the mirror, *"Man, I feel like I'm in a strange dream. It's surreal to think of Grace, kidnapped and a missing person halfway around the world. I don't know the guy she's with or if she's safe or even alive."*

He washed his face and hands. He reached for the comb in his pocket and slowly withdrew it, and tried to fix his hair. *"I could care less what my hair looks like for the next ten years if I lose my Grace. I've wasted this whole year getting closer and closer to her, and I never once told her that I was falling in love with her."*

He looked at his reflection as a wisp of hair fell over his left eye and stuck to his wet skin. He flipped it back up on his head with his comb and supposed, *"this looks fine!"*

As he walked to the door, he caught a glimpse of his hair again and thought, *"I'm a real idiot."*

Chapter 36

The group on the United States Cutter said their goodbyes to Philip. He prepared to meet up and transfer to one of the three United States Aircraft Carriers that patrol the Pacific Ocean. He'll fly to The Coast Guard Academy in New London, Connecticut.

Kate turned to Grace and said, "We need to work out a plausible, tight storyline that will save Philip's life. You'll need to tell no one that. When we arrive at the Tahiti Hilton Resort, you will have to perform a believable version of this story. You obviously had an incredible adventure combining your ride in a seaplane, the bird strike, your crash land on water, your climbing onto an uninhabitable island, and your ultimate survival for 2 nights and 3 days."

"Yes," replied Grace. "That has to make sense. My parents are here, at my request to see if that Victorian key fits the locket from the lighthouse cornerstone. This is a big deal to my family, and I don't want negative thoughts spoiling this wonderful adventure. I'd love it if I could arrange for them to stay for a week's vacation and soak up the memories of a lifetime. However, if the key doesn't fit, or they never found the cornerstone of the original lighthouse, I still want them to have a wonderful time."

Maggie agreed, "Yes, Let's make this as simple as possible. Let's see, we can have your pilot, Philip, be very helpful in all the survival projects. Nothing has to change on the first 2 days and nights."

Grace added, "What if we stick with the truth about the tide rising to unusual heights because of the Teahupoʻo surf on the southern coast of Tahiti? It was responsible for the enormous tides that caused the plane to get loose and float away. Then it comes back as it really did. You saw the empty seaplane that day and thought we hadn't survived. That's all true. The second night goes as it really did.

"This morning, after we made our coffee lattes and ate some coconut/pineapple mix, Philip took the seaplane down to the water to go for help as the waves took him out. He took some large palm branches to wave with if he saw any airplanes or boats. He did not return."

"That will be the end of my story as it really happened. No need to fabricate anything. Then you noticed my smoke signal and followed it here."

"Very good," exclaimed Maggie. "Kate and I can handle details of how we discovered the empty seaplane without survivors. That will clear Philip of any ongoing problems with the Cartel. He'll be safe and sound, on the other side of the world, and no longer at risk."

"Later, 'Antonio' will arrive in Sea Crest to head up the International Drug Enforcement Unit with me," Maggie finished with relief.

"Well," said Kate as she climbed into the helicopter. "It's time to get back to the Tahiti Hilton Resort."

Grace and Maggie boarded the aircraft, and the three best friends, who were halfway around the world from the Sea Crest Lighthouse, headed for the resort.

Chapter 37

The group from Sea Crest was gathered in the atrium of The Tahiti Hilton when Grace walked in with her survival kit backpack, coconuts, and the biggest smile of her life.

Her Mom and Dad ran up to her and smothered her with kisses, hugs, and tears. Granted, they had held it together pretty well up until they actually saw her, but they fell apart once they caught a glimpse of her.

Sarah said, "Grace, you look marvelous. We thought we might never see you again, Dear."

Grace explained, "I didn't think you knew I was missing. I didn't know you were worried about me. I'm so sorry."

Her dad's tearful hug said it all. "We left right after your phone call. I don't know all the details, but this is now a dream come true. Of course, it was a nightmare when we learned you were missing. We're so glad you're safe."

Mary Beth was the next to approach her, "Oh Grace, I was so afraid I'd never see you again!"

"Mary Beth! What are you doing here?"

"I wanted to share your Tahiti adventure with you. After I dropped you off at the airport, I returned home and packed. I arrived the next morning. I figure I landed after you left to go sightseeing in the seaplane."

"Wow, what a wonderful surprise!" Grace hugged her.

"Are you alright, Grace?" Mary Beth asked. She suddenly realized, *"Wow, she's never looked better. She looks like a healthy, tanned, thin version of my best friend."*

Jeffrey Williams joined them and added, "Wow! I'm so glad to see you. You really had us worried there, Grace."

"Jeffrey! What in the world are you doing here?" Grace was astonished to see him. "I hope James didn't ask you to come all the way to Tahiti! All I was asking for was some long-distance help with information on Captain James Cook and his connection to the Venus Pointe Lighthouse."

Jeffrey took the opportunity to hug Grace and confide, "Well, I have a couple of great reasons to be here. First, I have lots of unused vacation time, and second, I think Tahiti is a luxurious island paradise. I welcomed the opportunity to spend some time here."

"Yes, I agree; Tahiti is an unbelievably beautiful place. When I get settled, I'd love to talk with you about any information you can research about the repair of the Venus Pointe Lighthouse in 1965. I need to know about the cornerstone in the original lighthouse."

Jeff nodded, "Yes, I have a copy of all the details of that repair on my computer. I know you can't do anything this evening, but just say the word tomorrow. I'll be available to go over all my information."

"You're kidding," Grace exclaimed. "How did you do that so fast?"

"When James called me and explained what you needed, I knew I could help. I'm a board member of the Captain James Cook Society in New York City. I had their office forward the entire file on the 1965 repair of the Venus Pointe Lighthouse to my laptop. I also had them include an affidavit giving me the authority to review the contents of the cornerstone with the Sea Crest Historian, Grace Cook, present.

"Oh, that's wonderful! Let's meet tomorrow morning around ten o'clock. Then we can go to the lighthouse and possibly the museums in the afternoon."

Grace waved her parents back to join the conversation. "Mom and Dad, I'd like to introduce you to Attorney Jeffrey Williams from New York City. You probably saw him at Kate and Michael's wedding celebration. He's agreed to help us figure out a critical piece of the puzzle that developed when I opened the Sea Crest Lighthouse cornerstone a few days ago. I'll explain the timeline with the connection to the Venus Pointe Lighthouse tomorrow morning around ten o'clock. Can you both join us then?"

Grace's Dad said, "Of course. Is this why you wanted us to fly to Tahiti?"

"Yes, Dad. However, I'd like to share the whole story with you tomorrow. I'm suddenly kind of wiped out. I'd like to take a very long shower and get some sleep in one of the most comfortable beds in the entire world."

"Oh, of course!" said her mom. "I can only imagine how starved you must be. We can order room service for whatever you want."

"No, that's all taken care of. I got a cheeseburger and fries onboard the Coast Guard Cutter that was part of the rescue team. Kate had them standing by offshore. They thought we might need medical help, and we made a stop there for a wonderful meal in the Officer's Mess Hall."

"Well, where is the other part of the 'we'? I understand the seaplane pilot was with you. Where is he?" asked her father.

"He went for help in the yellow seaplane, taking coconut tree palms to wave in the air if a plane or boat came into view. We thought that would be more visible than anything we could do from shore. However, the waves took him out of sight. That's the last I saw of him."

"Wow, is that how Kate's SARS team found you?" asked Jeff.

"Well, no," Grace said sadly. She was so emotional after seeing her folks and Mary Beth, who had worried and prayed for her survival. It was easy to have tears in her eyes as she continued to recite the cover story, "We doubt that Philip survived."

Grace explained, "I was informed that they discovered the empty seaplane without any survivors. It had capsized near an atoll that would have been underwater at high tide. This is probably a direct result of the big wave surf break known as Teahupo'o along the south coast of Tahiti being in full force. It affects many of the islands and atolls in the area. In the world of big wave surfing, it's famous. Several times a year, elite athletes gather as monster swells form along the horizon and grow into the planet's most unique and previously "unrideable" waves. It wouldn't take much to overturn the little seaplane."

"Grace, I'm so sorry you had to go through this ordeal," said her mother, as she hugged her.

Grace considered, *"This ordeal was what led me to realize how much I love Joe. What did he feel when he heard I was missing? Was he even told that I was missing?"*

Now the tears really started to flow. *"What is Joe feeling now? Has he heard that I was rescued and that I'm okay?"*

Chapter 38

The following day Grace and her parents met Jeffrey Williams at the breakfast buffet.

Jeffery was on his second cup of coffee when he spotted Grace, and her folks enter the atrium set up with a bountiful brunch display. "Good morning," he said. "I hope you slept well."

Grace's father couldn't help but declare, "Boy, talk about a good night's sleep! I never realized these resorts all share similar terrific sleep systems. They've been adopted by Hilton's worldwide chain of hotels. The mattresses and box springs for their Serta Mattress Hilton Garden Inn, Serta Suite Dreams Hilton, Serenity, and other luxury brands. Their brochure explains you can purchase these for your home. It reads; 'Wake up each morning immersed in luxury with Hilton bedding, pillows, linens, comforters, and more. Shop Hilton.com.' These sleep sets can even be purchased on Amazon."

At that point, Mary Beth walked through the entrance and heard what he said. As she sat down, she added, "Plus, you never have to bring your own pillow on a trip. The pillowcases are labeled either hard or soft. Just pick your preference. They always have extras in the closet."

Grace noticed everyone had eaten their brunch and were just having coffee. At around 10 o'clock, she announced, "I think we should get started on why I asked you all to help me figure out the importance of what I found in the Sea Crest Lighthouse Cornerstone."

"First of all, I'd like to thank you, Mom and Dad, for dropping everything and coming to Tahiti. I'll explain the mystery in a minute."

Her dad smiled and said, "We are happy to come, and we're excited to hear what it's all about."

Next, Grace turned to Jeffrey, "And you," she laughed, "I never expected you to come. I appreciate all the help you can give me in figuring this puzzle out. Thank you!"

"And Mary Beth, I'm thrilled that you followed to join my adventure. You're the best!"

Grace opened the copy of the parchment that she chased down the Sea Crest Beach, "This is why we're all here. When I opened the Sea Crest Lighthouse cornerstone, one of the things I retrieved was a bottle, on which I cut my finger. I promptly dropped it over the side of the railing, and it smashed on the rocks below. The wind loosened a fragile piece of parchment, and I chased it down the beach until I could reach it. This is a copy of the parchment, which was rolled up inside and sealed displaying the RLS."

"Wow, is that who I think it is?" exclaimed Jeffrey in awe.

"Well, that depends on who you think it is," laughed Grace.

"Robert Louis Stevenson?"

"Yes! Isn't that amazing? Wait until you hear what this says," said Grace as she opened the copy. She began to read aloud, *"My father, Thomas Stevenson, drew up the plans to build the Tahiti Lighthouse on the site of Captain James Cook's observation conservatory. Our Stevenson family has retained close ties with Captain James Cook's Scottish family."*

Grace stopped reading and looked lovingly at her dad. "That's when I remembered that you had wanted to travel to Tahiti to view the 2014 phenomenon of the transit of Venus across the Sun. It was visible from Tahiti and French Polynesia and rarely occurred. This trip would have been a once-in-a-lifetime opportunity for you. But sadly, you could not actually make that trip. Still, we as a family continued researching Captain James Cook's voyages and The Islands of French Polynesia."

"My previous research had uncovered that Captain James Cook's ancestry line had many ancestors, including his own mother, named Grace."

She picked up the cherished letter again and continued reading. *"My grandfather placed a unique locket inside the hollowed-out cornerstone of The Pointe Venus Lighthouse. It's located on the northern tip of Tahiti in the Society Islands, French Polynesia. It was built in 1868. It is the key to a valuable keepsake locket, which holds a picture of Captain James Cook. The key will be passed down through future generations by the ancestors of the James Cook Family.*

In the future, when the cornerstone is recovered, and the locket is found, it can only be opened with the key that his ancestors possess. The locket has a picture of his mother, Grace Cook, and his father, James Cook, in a separate, hidden locket compartment. This secret opening can only be unlocked with the key. This will prove the lineage chain for their family when the cornerstone's locket is opened with the ancestor's key."

Grace softly said, "Dad, I was stunned as I vaguely wondered about the old Victorian key from your mother. I hadn't even thought about that key in ages. However, isn't it funny that we never did discover what that key opened?"

Her dad was sitting perfectly still as the whole possibility of these shocking events started to sink in. They might really be related to Captain James Cook!

Grace continued to explain, "Well, I stood there on the Sea Crest Beach, and I couldn't believe it, but I couldn't help but think, maybe it was. After all, it was just too wild to even think about. I was sure grandma's key was 'not' this mysterious ancestral connection to Captain James Cook's family. After all, it's been among several pieces of costume jewelry of no significant value that was kept inside her jewelry box. Dad's family certainly wasn't wealthy by any means. We eventually agreed that Grandma found the beautiful 'orphan' trinket with the pretty blue stones was too pretty to part with, even if it didn't fit anything."

Grace concluded, "I just couldn't live with myself if I didn't try to discover the truth."

The silence was deafening as Grace turned to her mother and asked, "Mom, did you bring the Victorian key?"

Sarah Cook slid the folded handkerchief out of her purse and unwrapped the Victorian key. The aquamarine jewels shimmered and sparkled in the light.

Grace explained, "The history of aquamarine stones goes way back. In fact, there is evidence of aquamarine being worn by the Ancient Romans as well as Ancient Egyptians, proving that this striking blue stone has been loved for centuries. Aquamarines are far more expensive when compared to Topaz or other stones. Derived from Latin words meaning 'seawater,' these gemstones have a brief history of being considered sacred in the Roman and Greek empires. Decorative aquamarine jewelry dating back to 500BC has been found. This discovery proves that this striking gemstone was just as popular then as it is in jewelry today. The aquamarine has an interesting history with many beliefs and superstitions tied to it."

Her mother asked, "What do you mean?"

Grace said, "The belief that aquamarine can protect its wearer dates back centuries. The gemstone was often worn by sailors as it was believed to help bring them safely home.

"Ancient Romans and other societies believed the stone had healing properties and used it to treat various ailments.

"Some cultures believed aquamarine could increase youth, intelligence, foresight, courage, and happiness. Wearing this gemstone was thought to bring the wearer many good things. However, the Romans took a slightly different approach, instead using the stone to treat maladies. Aquamarine was thought to cure liver, stomach, and throat issues.

"I think that it was considered good luck for sailors. According to myth, it was believed that the Roman God, Neptune, found the first aquamarine gemstone washed up on the shore, where it fell out of his jewelry box. It is thought that Neptune would not want to lose aquamarine stones to the sea, so he would protect the sailors that wore the gemstone."

Jeffery asked, "May I take a look?"

As she carefully handed the key to him, he inspected it thoroughly. "This is exactly true to the time when Tiffany made jewelry in what people called his Blue period. He loved the look and color of these aquamarine stones. Louis Comfort Tiffany also used the aquamarine color in many art pieces and stained glass pieces. In fact, he chose this color for the little blue Tiffany boxes. You are holding an original key made by Tiffany. Yes, I'm sure it's the one that opens the locket, which I'll personally guarantee, was made by Tiffany also."

Sarah remarked, "It's such an iconic shade of blue."

Jeffery smiled and continued, "Yes, it's famous. Charles Tiffany and John Young created the medium robin egg color in 1837. In 1845 the New York City jewelry company used the blue color on the cover of Tiffany's Blue Book. Since then, Tiffany & Co. has used the color extensively on promotional materials like boxes and bags."

"Since 1998, the Tiffany Blue® color has been registered as a color trademark by Tiffany & Co. It was standardized in 2001 as a custom color created by Pantone® exclusively for Tiffany and is not publicly available. This color was called "1837 Blue," named after Tiffany's founding year."

Jeffrey handed the beautiful key back to Sarah Cook as he remarked, "Tiffany jewelry, including this key, is truly an international icon of elegance! I'm thrilled that I have the opportunity to see it."

Grace thought, *"I'm so glad I invited my parents to join me as I continue to find out if the Robert Louis Stevenson parchment letter is valid."*

"I can hardly wait to see what we find out about the cornerstone of the lighthouse," she said. "I hope we can get in to see everything today."

Chapter 39

Grace was on cloud nine as she suggested, "Next, we need to head out to the Venus Pointe Lighthouse. I'll explain the details as soon as we get a vehicle and driver to help us get around the island."

The resort manager stepped forward with a couple of young men. "Ms. Cook, please let me introduce you to a couple of fellows who may be able to help you."

"First, let me introduce Jacques. He is the finest chauffeur in Tahiti."

Jacques stepped forward and shook her hand, "Bonjour, mademoiselle."

The manager continued, "He is extremely interested in The Venus Pointe Lighthouse's history and Captain James Cook's legacy. Jacques has asked to help you in any way possible. It would be our pleasure to offer his services."

"Now, this is Pierre. He is the island's Tahitian historian and guide. He speaks fluent English and knows the managers for both the Venus Pointe Lighthouse and the Museums."

Pierre stepped forward, took Grace's hand, and said, "Bonjour, mademoiselle Cook. It's a pleasure to meet you."

The manager continued, "We at the Hilton Tahiti Resort are prepared to help you in any way possible. It would be our pleasure to offer the services of both of these professionals. They are yours for your entire stay, compliments of the resort."

"Thank you so much," said Grace. "Well, we'd like to go to the Venus Pointe Lighthouse first and see if they recovered the cornerstone when they repaired the lighthouse in 1965. We'll let you know the details once we're on the road."

"Let me introduce my parents, James, and Sarah Cook. This is Mary Beth, one of my best friends. And this gentleman is Attorney Jeffrey Williams. He's on the board of the Captain James Cook Society in New York City. He has the information from the Captain James Cook Society archives about the repair of the lighthouse in 1965. He will be able to access these on his laptop."

As they loaded up and got situated, they had plenty of room to spread out. "Thank you both for your help! This is much better than what we had in mind," Grace said.

"Since our first stop will be The Venus Pointe Lighthouse, which happens to be the northernmost place of Tahiti," Grace continued, "We can each share what we know about it. On April 13th, 1769, Captain James Cook arrived in Tahiti aboard de Endeavour to observe Venus' transit, planned on June 3rd. This expedition aimed to calculate the distance between the Sun and the Earth. Today, James Cook's notes remain one of the most prolific sources of information regarding the past Polynesian society."

"Before Captain James Cook's arrival:

"March 5th, 1797: English missionaries from the London Missionary Society (LMS) accosted Matavai Bay aboard the Duff and settled in Point Venus.

"In 1851, the application was filed to have a sidereal lantern built on the Point Venus site."

"What is that?" asked James Cook.

Jeffrey answered, "I've learned about some of the early equipment pieces used in this period. I believe a sidereal is an astronomical time system like a sundial for the night sky. A timekeeper is an instrument or person that measures the passage of time. So if you find a celestial object at a certain position at a specific time on one night, you can look for it again the next night."

Jeffrey continued, "In 1856, The sidereal was finally installed.

"August 1867: An application was filed to build a lighthouse on the site.

"It was approved on April 12th, 1864, and it was finally built by August 1867."

Grace continued, "It is reported to have been built by Thomas Stevenson, father of author Robert Louis Stevenson."

"Yes," agreed Jeffrey Williams. He looked through the information on his laptop and read, *"Designed by Thomas Stevenson (1818-1887), father of the author Robert Louis Stevenson and a member of Scotland's famous family of lighthouse builders."*

"It also says; *Robert Louis Stevenson visited the lighthouse with Thomas' widow in 1888. A plaque above the entrance recorded: 'Great were my feelings of emotion as I stood with my mother by my side. We looked at the edifice designed by my father when I was sixteen and worked in his office during the summer of 1866.'*

"This lighthouse remains the only one in Tahiti. It's generally known as "Teara o Tahiti" in reo Maohi. Its square tower of 8 floors 25 meters high was edified of rubble stone and corals by Thomas Stevenson, helped by masons from Mangareva."

Jeffrey explained, "Mangareva is the largest island of the Gilbert Islands, which are part of French Polynesia. However, they are about 1,000 miles southeast of Tahiti."

"The lighthouse was finally lit on New Year's Day, January 1st, 1868.

"During World War II, 1939 to 1945, Mahina's citizens (the city where the lighthouse is located) painted coconut trees on their

lighthouse to hide it and prevent the Japanese fleet from landing in Tahiti.'"

Grace said, "Thank you, Jeffrey. Now, can you check your archive records for the date of the repairs? I have two conflicting dates:

"The first one says,1953: One floor was added to elevate the lighthouse, to make it easier to be seen."

"The second says, 1963: Refurbished and raised in height by 7 m (23 ft) in 1963. That's the date on everything else I could verify. What do you think?"

Jeffrey searched through the records and agreed, "I agree. It looks like they are describing the same repair event to refurbish and raise the height by adding one floor to elevate the height. They mistakenly recorded the 1953 date in error."

"I agree," said Grace. "It was finished in 1965. I also show that it was only electrified in 1973. After being forsaken for about 50 years because of Papeete's harbor development, Point Venus regained popularity with foreigners and now attracts more and more tourists yearly.

"Today, the Point Venus lighthouse still operates and testifies to the evolution of the Pacific history. It is also used for aerial navigation as lenses for aerial clusters were added."

Now, Grace wanted to know what the Tahitians from the hotel thought. "Pierre, as the island's Tahitian historian and guide, what do you think of our information so far? Does it sound correct to you?"

Pierre said, "Yes, I've been following everything you've said so far, and I think you also have the correct date when the refurbishing and repair were done, once in 1963-1965. We can double-check when we arrive at the lighthouse.

"I'd also like to add that when Robert Louis Stevenson visited the lighthouse in 1868, he requested that a plaque be added to honor his father's design and work in the lighthouse. We can see it today.

"Point Venus has a substantial black sand beach, beautiful azure water, her storybook Victorian lighthouse, and a long and fabled history. It's a charming place, which everyone enjoys visiting.

"Point Venus is the symbol of the encounter of Europeans and Polynesians, a place where you can meander and stroll the grounds, surf or learn about Polynesian history."

Grace smiled as she said, "Thank you, Pierre, for your help. Now we have to see if they found the cornerstone RLS wrote and places in the Sea Crest Lighthouse over 100 years ago."

Mary Beth couldn't help but comment on the beautiful scenery they saw on the drive. "This is absolutely the most beautiful place on earth! How far is the lighthouse from here? I hope we'll be able to talk with someone there."

Grace agreed, "Yes, I hope someone is available to ask about the cornerstone."

Pierre spoke up, "I've arranged for the managers of the lighthouse and the museum to meet with us today. They are eager to talk with you."

Jacque announced, "We should be at the lighthouse in about 5 minutes."

Chapter 40

Meanwhile, at the airport passport expedite office, Joe arrived bright and early, trying to complete his US Passport application packet with the staff's help. His ticket was for this evening's flight; he had to finalize everything and hope the special delivery service worked.

Late last night, they had taken his picture and processed several transactions, along with the forms of payment.

Joe to keep them up to date on the situation of Grace missing. He told her that he was flying out to Tahiti and his problem of having no passport and the expedited service he was using to remedy the situation.

While they were at it, he asked his mom, "I assume you'll be out running errands today. I'd like to ask you for a favor."

"Of course; what do you need?"

"Well, this will sound really stupid, but I've recently realized that I've got very deep and somewhat surprising feelings for Grace!"

His mom almost burst out laughing as she rolled her eyes. For the past year, Grace has been all he's talked about. She calmly asked him, "Why, what do you mean, Dear? I do believe you've mentioned her to us."

He quickly relayed the events of the last couple of days to her. He finished with, "You know, Mom, I was in court and didn't even know she'd left for Tahiti until late in the day. I received her message to call her, and I wasn't even upset then."

"Well, Joe, she had left you a message when she realized that you were unavailable until you could place the call to her. It wasn't that she was keeping anything from you."

"I know, and I was absolutely fine with all that. It's just that when I called her, I was put on hold for a long time. I started thinking about Grace being so far away from me. I mean, we were always accessible to talk or get together. I felt strangely upset that I hadn't gone with her to share the trip. She's halfway around the world, and I really miss her."

"Well," explained his mom softly. "It's not unusual to miss someone suddenly gone when you've been practically inseparable for months. Have you two talked about how close you've become?"

"Of course not! We didn't even know it had happened! Now I feel so upset! What if I never see Grace again? I never even told her I loved her! How did I let this happen? What was I thinking?"

"Okay, hopefully, they will find Grace and her pilot, and you'll get the chance to tell her how much she means to you." She quickly added, "Do not forget to tell her that you love her. I'm sure she feels the same way, but you must tell her, my dear son."

"You really think she feels the same?" he asked in astonishment.

"Yes, however, we're not mind readers," she laughed.

Joe was very serious as he broached the next subject. "Mom, that brings me to the next logical step. I must get a chance to see Grace. I've been trying to get to Tahiti for three days now. Everything seems to cause a delay, but I need to reach her. I hope and pray she'll be safe and sound when I arrive." His voice broke as he admitted, "If they haven't found her, I don't know what I'll do."

His mom said, "We are all praying. Is there anything else we can do?"

After a moment, Joe said, "Yes, mom. I'd like to ask you about something we talked about long ago. However, I think you might agree."

"What? Anything you need, the answer is Yes!"

Joe said, "Do you remember talking with me about what was in your safe deposit box? It was soon after I got my Law Degree. You were so proud of my achievements. You were going on and on joking about all the business you and Dad were going to give me. Like that was going to get me afloat while I started my law office, completely ignoring how much the extra cost for law school had been."

"Yes, I vaguely recall something like that," she laughed.

"Well, I remember you showing me Grandma's Art Nouveau wedding ring and her wish to keep it in the family. I once described it to Grace when we discussed her Grandmother's key that they held in their safe deposit box. They had no idea what it was supposed to open. Still, the Aquamarine jewels on the keepsake were beautiful, and the family's sentimental value meant everything to them.

"Grace is a historian by trade and a lover of history by choice. We had a long discussion on the changes in jewelry from the Victorian Era through the Art Nouveau and on to Art Deco. I'd love to ask for her hand in marriage if she loves me too. If you agree, I'd be honored to put Grandma's ring on Grace's finger for our engagement ring."

"Oh, Joe, that's a wonderful gesture," cried his mother. "Yes! I couldn't be happier and know your grandma would love it!"

"Thanks," Joe replied.

His mom added, "I'll pick it up at the bank. Can one of those super fast couriers you're bragging about pick it up? Be sure you insure it when you fly. I'll include the appraisal certificate."

Joe was surprised. "Mom, what's that about? Is that ring valuable?"

"Oh, you'll see! I'll have it all ready for the courier service to pick up within the hour," she said as she rang off.

Joe turned to the assistant helping him and marveled in awe, "Well, that's a surprise! My mom is sending my grandmother's engagement ring for me to use when I propose to the 'love of my life.'"

"Congratulations!" said the young man. He was filling out the final check list.

"Thanks," replied Joe. He felt like his heart was going to leap out of his chest.

"Next," said the clerk, checking off the boxes for the necessary steps. "We need to verify that you have a copy of a valid ticket for tonight to travel to Tahiti. - Yes!

"We need the emergency contact. Yes, we have that - You are using your mother and father.

"Now we need to recheck the processes of all the various forms of payment for each document and organization has been successful."

While the aide typed the information into the laptop, Joe tried to call Grace's cell phone with no luck.

Joe worried as he looked at the failure notice. His calls and texts didn't even complete the contact. *"It's like the phone is completely dead. Maybe it is broken or has water in it."*

Chapter 41

As Jacque drove the limo along the beach road and parklike setting, they arrived at the northern tip of Tahiti. At last, the tall, white, beautiful Pointe Venus Lighthouse came into view.

Jacque pulled up to the Victorian structure and announced, "Welcome to the famous Pointe Venus Lighthouse. The manager, Mr. Teva, is the smiling man coming to meet us."

He exited the driver's seat and opened the doors for them. Pierre and Jacque were the first to shake hands with Mr. Teva, who was a long-time friend of theirs. Pierre then introduced Grace and her parents, James and Sarah Cook. "They traveled a long way to discover what might have happened to the cornerstone of this lighthouse during the 1963 renovations. If it was found, they believe it holds proof that they are ancestors of Captain James Cook."

He continued, "This is Attorney Jeffrey Williams, on the board of The Captain James Cook Society in New York City. He had their office forward the entire file on the 1965 repair of the Venus Pointe Lighthouse to his laptop. They also sent an affidavit giving Jeffrey Williams the authority to review the contents of the cornerstone with the Sea Crest Historian, Grace Cook, present."

"Wow," said the manager. "It's an honor to meet someone from The Captain James Cook Society. I am completely at your service. Hopefully, you will also be able to help us verify some historical questions that we've always wondered about."

Pierre also introduced Mary Beth, "She's a close friend of Grace. She has been to France and is greatly interested in French Polynesia."

Mr. Teva stated, "I've also invited Ms. Alana Flores, The Museum of Tahiti and the Islands curator, to join us today. She is interested in all you have to share and will help you in any way possible."

She smiled and said, "Hello, it's a pleasure to meet you this morning! I'll be delighted to take you to the museum after we discuss the Venus Pointe Lighthouse."

"It would be helpful, and we appreciate your help," stated Jeffrey Williams.

They continued to talk their cordial conversation under the coconut trees, with the ocean breezes making the morning ideal.

Grace explained, "This note from RLS that was found in the cornerstone at the Sea Crest Lighthouse. That led us to The Venus Pointe Lighthouse, built in 1868 and renovated in the 1960s. Now we need to know if the locket was found in the cornerstone of the original lighthouse."

"Amazing!" exclaimed Alana.

"If a locket was found, we need to see if my mother-in-law's Victorian key will fit and open to reveal a picture of Captain Cook's parents," said Sarah Cook.

"That will prove the ancestry line of Captain James Cook leads to my family," said James Cook proudly.

"Yes," said Alana, "The cornerstone was found. The contents are in The Musée de Tahiti et des Îles, The Museum of Tahiti, and the Islands. We can view the contents today."

"Wonderful," said Grace.

Alana smiled and explained, "First, I'd like to show you where the time capsule was found." They stepped over to an area a few feet away from the lighthouse's base.

"The workers had disrupted much of the land surrounding the lighthouse. The rubble was piled several feet deep in some places. Several weeks into the project, the workers found an old wooden box with a smaller sealed metal box inside. It was discarded for an additional week because nobody realized it might hold something of real value. It just looked like junk."

"Wow, that's unbelievable!" murmured Jeffrey.

Alana laughed, "Well, here in French Polynesia, it's not so strange. The Lighthouse was designed and built by the Scottish lighthouse builder, Thomas Stevenson. It was built at Venus Point in Mahina, the only lighthouse in Tahiti with more than a century and a half of life. It is, for 150 years, still in activity and today completely automated. At 32.85 meters and 365 steps in height, this large building, built in 1867 and inaugurated on April 23rd, 1868, watches over the north coast of Tahiti."

Mr. Teva stated, "Venus Point was named in memory of Captain Cook's mission in 1769, whose goal was to observe the planet Venus. The lighthouse was built in 1867 by workers from the island of Mangareva. They used stones and rubble from farms and the coral and sand of the archipelago of Gambier. Indeed they are the only ones to know how to build stone buildings. They were known for erecting hundreds of stone religious churches and buildings in Gambier. This includes the cathedral of Papeete.

"The Venus Point Lighthouse has served its duty for 150 years, except during the 1939-1945 war. Since it was located in a coconut grove, they painted coconut trees on all four faces of the lighthouse. In this way, it was camouflaged from the enemy fleet and could no longer serve as a landmark.

"The Pointe Venus lighthouse is today protected and maintained by the Department of Lights and Beacons of the Equipment Service. It was the first lighthouse in the South Pacific!

"The Polynesian Post illustrated a commemorative stamp for the 150th anniversary of the inauguration of the Venus Point lighthouse.

"On the subject of cornerstones, they aren't connected to any particular group, either secular or non-secular. Although it's common for them to be laid in buildings such as educational facilities, libraries, and social and community centers. I think the traditional churches used the cornerstone with the idea that the ruling principles of the church are rooted in a strong foundation.

"The laying of cornerstones is not linked to any one group. Traditionally churches placed cornerstones with the idea that the ruling principles of the church are rooted in a strong foundation. However, placing cornerstones does not appear to be linked to only non-secular organizations. It is common for cornerstones to be laid in buildings such as libraries, educational facilities, and social and community organizations. Those which are meant to be opened on a specific date and those that are not. A large celebration such as a World Fair or raising a new building often encourages people to lay a time capsule.

"This newly created desire to preserve their valuable past was also heightened because these people had lived through the industrial revolution, which seemed to speed time up. Many sought to view the past as a safe refuge from the hectic and rough present.

"The Victorian era gave rise to autobiography, journaling, and diary writing. In fact, it was seen as their responsibility to document the past. This recording of time is also demonstrated by time capsules."

They stepped into the lighthouse to get out of the sun. Alana said, "Now we come to the subject of time capsules. They have been used for thousands of years to preserve a piece of the present for the future. They, of course, are not the magnificent shiny chest full of buried treasure that is most dreamed of. However, there are four distinct types. They can either be intentional or unintentional. They can also be those which are meant to be opened on a specific date and those that are not.

"One example of an unintentional type is the city of Pompeii, Italy. The ancient roman city was buried under 13 - 20 ft of volcanic ash and pumice when Mount Vesuvius erupted in 79 AD. The town was primarily preserved under the ash, as it was at the time it was the time of the eruption.

"Another example happened during the Victorian era (1837 to 1901) when the first remains of the Neanderthals were discovered. These were their first discoveries, including bodies, tools, and artifacts unearthed from a period that existed before their present understanding of time. A new understanding of time evolved from this era.

"Intentional time capsules have been criticized by historians as they do not provide much useful historical data. Useless items include outdated technology or unused, pristine items. More useful items are photos and documents that describe everyday life. The second critique of intentional time capsules concerns preservation problems. Papers often disintegrate, groundwater destroys buried capsules, and the time capsule's precise location can be lost over time. While the critique suggests that time capsules may not accurately represent society, they can give us valuable information. The societal ideas of time and the importance of particular objects are illustrated in the contents of the time capsules we find today.

"In the Victorian era, there was a societal shift in which more emphasis was placed on the importance of time commemoration. The creation of a time capsule is an example of how people of the Victorian era commemorated time. Time capsules can be found in many cornerstones of buildings built in the Victorian era in Victoria, British Columbia. The content of each time capsule varies; however, the 'usual deposits' include coins, newspapers, and religious or historical statements. These objects show us the importance of religion and prosperity during the era. They also give us a glimpse into the Victorian understanding of time. These had no intended retrieval date and were expected to endure until the apocalypse.

"The word 'time capsule' was first used in 1937 when a capsule was prepared for burial for the 1939 New York World's Fair. However, the notion of the time capsule is much older. The idea of leaving a message for the future in a time capsule is more than 5,000 years old.

"Today, we are very familiar with the idea of leaving a piece of ourselves for a future civilization. Time capsules are used as a way of communicating with distant people. In fact, there are currently two-time capsules in space. Voyager Golden Records I and II were attached to two Voyager spacecraft and launched in 1977. Music, natural sounds, images from around the world, and greetings in 55 languages are included on the record. This is an example of a time capsule with an unknown opening date.

"The time capsule found here from The Venus Pointe Lighthouse original site was definitely intentional. When we discovered the old box located inside a stone enclosure. It was at ground level, surrounded by fill and other construction material. Workers pulled off the top of the stone enclosure to find the box, which appeared to be made of copper, sitting in water.

"The box was then covered in protective wrapping and, for safety, was transported by vehicle from the site to the museum for further study. It wasn't clear what condition the contents would be in. As a precaution, it took a while to get it open."

"I'd love to accompany you all over to the museum and show you the contents of what we found," finished Alana.

Chapter 42

Joe was notified that the courier had arrived in time with his passport. "Wow, I'm so glad you could get this processed for me. I really appreciate what you've done for me!

"Now, I want to see if my documents from my mom have arrived."

"Yes, it's all right here. Plus an extraordinary piece of jewelry," said his aide, Charles.

As Joe unwrapped his grandmother's engagement ring, he was touched that this was such a stunning ring. *"This certificate that mom enclosed tells exactly why it needs to be insured."*

This is a 2.90 Carat Diamond Engagement Ring – European-cut Diamond

Rows of small Swiss-cut diamonds – Total diamond weight 3.45 carats

GIA Diamond Grading Report

G Color

VS1 clarity,

Late Edwardian/ Early Art Deco

Platinum over Gold

Round Brilliant

Size 6

Appraised Value: $65,000.00

He showed it to Charley, who whistled and promptly filled out and processed the insurance transaction. Charley stated, "Well, my friend, you're good to go! Your flight leaves in 30 minutes! It was a pleasure working with you!"

"What do you mean? My flight doesn't leave for a few hours."

"Well, I just got a call from the airline. They have a flight taking off in 30 minutes. They are substituting the regularly scheduled aircraft for one that can fly non-stop to Tahiti. Since most passengers are ready to go, they're saving your seat until you get there."

"Wow, I'll have to run!"

"No problem! We have a driver standing by outside the front door with an electric passenger transport cart. He'll drive our special company transport cart directly to your gate."

"Thanks!" Joe said as he ran to the door to climb on the cart.

When he arrived at the gate, the Passenger Service Agent exchanged his ticket and checked him in. She was the same person who told him how to get a passport for the next day. She smiled as she congratulated him, "Glad you could make it, Mr. Lawrence. I see you were able to get your passport. It's your lucky day. You've just been upgraded to First Class compliments of our airline and the passport company. Enjoy your flight!"

"Thank you," he replied as he hurried down the jetway to board the plane.

The door slammed closed behind him.

As he got settled in his new incredible First Class seat, he finally thought things were improving for him. *"Now, if only I could find that Grace is safe and sound when I arrive at Tahiti."*

After a smooth take-off and a terrific meal, Joe realized he was exhausted. He thought, *"This is a great time to lie back in my 180-degree flat-bed seat, with direct aisle access and close to the privacy wall. It's like a safe cacoon, with the softest pillows and a warm cozy blanket.*

"Granted, I've never been on a long flight like this before; however, I'm shocked by the sheer level of comfort.

"If only I knew Grace was safe. I'll try one more time to get ahold of her."

As he dialed her cell phone number, he felt heartsick. He knew it was not going to connect. He was right!

Joe hadn't slept for over 30 hours, and at this point, total exhaustion took its toll. Joe leaned back against the airline pillow, closed his tired eyes, and fell into a deep sleep.

Chapter 43

It was a short drive in the limousine to The Museum of Tahiti and the Islands. They were once again impressed by the magnificent beauty around them.

After a few minutes, they turned into the winding driveway and stepped out at the museum's entrance. Alana introduced them to the museum staff and workers. "We are so honored to have you visit with us today. We have some refreshments set up for you in the lobby area."

"We are closed to the public for the event of your memorable visit today. We wanted you to feel free to explore and discover what we found. Our Museum is divided into four sections, covering nature and anthropology, habitations and artifacts, social and religious life, and the history of French Polynesia.

"We have several artifacts and plaques in French and English to describe the objects.

"You're welcome to look around and talk with the staff.

"We have laid out the contents and documentation of the time capsule on these tables and shelves. I have something special in my office that I'll get to show you now."

Alana smiled and turned back to say, "Hopefully, we can solve your mystery about the key that you brought and your incredible connection to Captain James Cook."

Grace was both excited and apprehensive about the results of this excursion, traveling halfway around the world. *"What if they don't have a locket? What if the key doesn't fit? What if I got my dad's hopes up, and he's disappointed?"*

Alana returned and joined them after a few minutes. She was wearing white gloves and holding something in her hands. She walked over to Sarah Cook and whispered, "Do you think this might be the locket?"

Alana opened her hands to reveal a gold locket. Everyone gasped as Sarah, James, and Grace Cook gazed hopefully at the locket.

Grace exclaimed, "Alright, the moment of truth. Let's see if your key fits, Mom!"

Sarah stepped closer and held the key out to Alana. However, Alana shook her head, whispering, "Go ahead, you try it."

Sarah carefully took the beautiful key and inserted it into the lock of the locket that hadn't been opened for over one hundred years. It had a secret edge that had to be turned backward, but, at last, it opened. There was the picture of James Cook, and in a secret hidden compartment, a picture of his mother, Grace Cook, and his father, James Cook.

Sarah dropped down in a nearby chair with tears of joy. She handed the locket to James, who had his own tears rolling down his cheeks.

James was overcome with emotion as he looked at the long sought-after proof that he was descended from Captain James Cook. "Look! It's just as you described," he showed Grace.

"When I open the locket," he continued. "The top picture is of Captain James Cook, but hidden underneath are pictures of his father, James Cook, and his mother, Sarah Cook. This is truly the most significant revelation of my life. I never in my wildest dreams thought it could be proven. Thank you, Grace, for putting this together and making it possible for us to be able to share this moment."

Grace answered tearfully, "I was praying that Grandma's key would open the locket. When I read Robert Louis Stevenson's message, I recognized it was written in his own hand, with his own RLS seal. I knew it could be real."

Grace joyfully stated, "How lucky are we that we live at The Sea Crest Lighthouse? All the contacts were in place for Robert Louis Stevenson to know Sir Michael Chambers from Scotland."

Her father proudly added, "How lucky are we that you, my dear daughter, are the Sea Crest Historian?"

Chapter 44

With trembling fingers, he dialed the Tahiti Hilton Resort. "They were not going to get away with this!"

"Hello, The Tahiti Hilton Resort. How may I help you?"

"I need to speak with the manager, Mr. Allaire!"

"One moment Sir!"

Within a minute, the phone was answered, "Hello, this is the manager. How may I help you?"

"This is Attorney Joe Lawrence. I want to know."

Mr. Allaire cut him off, "Wait! Wait! Grace is alright! She's here!"

"What? You mean she's okay?"

"Yes,"

"Well, let me talk to her!"

"Well, she's not here right now. She went with her parents to the lighthouse, I think. They should be back soon."

"Great! My flight just landed. I'll be there soon myself, and Grace better be safe and unharmed, or you'll be sorry!"

Chapter 45

Grace was elated at the outcome of the Venus Pointe Lighthouse cornerstone's contents which proved her father was a direct descendant of the James Cook Family. She thought, *"I'm also thrilled that they presented the locket to my father. As a direct descendant of Captain James Cook, Alana and Jeffrey Williams agreed it would be appropriate to honor my father in this way.*

"That is what I'd hoped and prayed for, but my excitement is somehow missing something. I wish Joe was part of this adventure. I'm just not the same without him. It's like I'm not whole.

"Wow, that's scary! Does that mean that maybe I won't be truly happy again if Joe doesn't love me? What should I do?

"If I tell him how I feel and he doesn't feel the same way, will he want to end our friendship? Is that worth the risk? How can I go on without him in my life?"

Grace's mom looked over at her and softly asked, "Are you alright, honey?"

"Yes, of course. I guess I'm just a little tired. A whole lot has happened in the last few days. It's a lot to take in."

"Boy, you can say that again," she agreed with a nod.

Grace quickly explained, "Oh, I'm thrilled that you and Dad could drop everything and come to Tahiti."

"I'm still in shock!" added her dad vaguely. It was almost like he was far away, turning the whole episode over in his mind.

Grace started to laugh as she took his hand. "Isn't it wild? We are related to Captain James Cook! The whole thing is so unbelievable! I mean, really! And Robert Louis Stevenson, of all people. I've read hundreds of his letters in volumes of books spanning decades. He wrote to other authors, relatives, friends, and acquaintances. And now, low and behold, he wrote a letter to us! It's just wild!"

Grace wiped her laughing eyes and finished her outburst with, "Yes, it's unbelievable!"

But she was still thinking, *"I've just had the most monumental week of my life, and Joe is nowhere in sight. Yes, that's extremely sad and unbelievable."*

Chapter 46

Joe arrived at The Venus Pointe Hilton Resort and stepped away from the taxi with his suitcase. He searched for Grace as he hurried into the open-air lobby and headed straight for the check-in area. He turned around when he heard a big commotion behind him as a limousine pulled up to unload people.

That's when he saw Grace. He started for her, waving his arms and calling, "Grace! Grace!"

She heard that familiar voice and her heart leaped as she saw him. She waved and ran to him. "Joe! I'm so glad you're here!"

They met at the entrance, and both started talking simultaneously.

"Are you really okay, Grace?"

"Well, I am now! I'm surprised to see you. I didn't know you were coming!"

Grace celebrated and practically yelled, "Hey, everyone! Look, Joe's here!"

Joe was surprised to see all the people that were here. Then he spotted someone else he was surprised to see. *"Oh no! There's Jeffrey Williams. What's he doing here?"*

Joe realized that he was holding Grace's hand. He wasn't sure when that happened, but he wasn't letting go. He said, "Grace,

I was so worried about you. When I called, the manager told me you were kidnapped or something. How did you get away? Are you hurt? Where is that maniac?"

At the same time, Grace tried unsuccessfully to tell him, "I'm fine, I wasn't hurt, and I missed you."

However, they were interrupted by everyone coming to greet them and talk with Grace about the key. Did it open the locket? Was the locket the one from Captain James Stevenson's family?

Joe went over to the reception front desk and officially checked in.

Manager Allaire said, "I know you were extremely worried about Ms. Grace Cook. I'm sorry, I didn't know she was okay then. When she was rescued, and I could see that she appeared fine, I assumed she had been in contact with you."

"Yes, I can understand why you would think that."

Joe finished checking in. He gave his room number and a tip to the bell boy and directed him to take his luggage up to his room.

He glanced over to see Jeffrey Williams actively participating in the current conversation.

Joe felt a dark cloud come over him as he realized, *"Maybe Grace doesn't have romantic feelings for me, after all. How could I feel so much, and she doesn't feel anything?"*

Chapter 47

Maggie had heard about Joe Lawrence's demanding that the management of The Tahiti Hilton would be held responsible if anything happened to Grace. He was threatening a lawsuit and was extremely upset. As she entered the lobby, Maggie wondered, "Where is Dear Old Joe anyway?

She scanned the open-air atrium. Finally, she saw Joe deep in conversation with Attorney Jeffery Williams, and he didn't look too happy. As she approached them, Joe ran his hand through his hair with utter impatience and annoyance. He raised his hands in frustration and helplessly ended with his hands on his hips as he glared at Jeff.

Maggie arrived in the nick of time and stated with a cheery greeting, "Hey, I've been looking for you guys! What's up?"

Joe stopped to look at her in confusion. He brought one hand back to cradle his chin as though in deep thought. His throat felt like sandpaper, and his ears ached as he wondered why this hurt so much. "Well," he rasped as he scuffed his foot on the marble floor.

Maggie and Jeff continued to observe this display with concern. Jeff thought, *"Boy, I sure didn't see this side of Joe Lawrence back at Sea Crest. However, he cut in on me when I danced with Grace at Kate and Michael's wedding celebration."*

Jeff decided to let Maggie figure out what was going on with Joe, so he picked up a few finger sandwiches from the refreshment table and strolled away from the area.

Maggie had her own thoughts, *"Man, I've known Joe for years. He is the best attorney in the Sea Crest area. This looks serious."* She asked, "Joe, are you okay? Can I get you a glass of water?"

Joe shook his head and tried to calm down. After a moment, he cleared his dry throat and painfully declared, "I'm just trying to figure out why My Grace asked Jeff to fly all the way to Tahiti to join her."

Joe looked ready to explode!

Maggie said, "She didn't ask him. She didn't even talk to him. She asked me to have James talk with Jeffrey because he knew him from New York City. And asked if he had any information on the history of Captain James Cook and the Venus Pointe Lighthouse repair job in the 1960s.

"He might have access to online information in New York that it would be hard for her to locate from Tahiti.

"None of us had any idea that he would be on the board of the James Cook Society. We were all shocked when he showed up here."

Joe struggled with that for a while, then explained to Maggie, "When I saw Jeff here, I guess I Lost it! Did you see him dancing with her at Kate and Michael's Wedding Celebration?"

"No, I guess I was too involved with James that evening," she laughed.

He smiled, "Oh yeah. That's an understatement."

Maggie said, "Joe, I'm serious about Grace. She had no wish and no idea he would surprise her and come to Tahiti."

"Thanks, Maggie."

He scanned the room until he saw Grace and decided, *"Well, if Grace didn't ask Jeff to join her in Tahiti, Then Game On!"*

Chapter 48

Grace looked around the atrium and saw Joe walking toward her. His eyes never left her as he got closer. She took an unsteady step and supported herself by grasping a palm branch from the nearest artificial tree. It was one of the portable decorative trees that had been brought in for privacy. Well, that's exactly what it provided for them as Joe reached her.

He said, "Ah, Grace. I need to talk with you if you have a minute."

Grace wondered what was going on as she replied, "Of course, I know things got crazy there for a while when we walked in. They were all excited about our trip to the lighthouse and museum to see if the locket was found when they repaired the lighthouse."

She could see how solemn and hurt he looked. So she added, "However, I heard you ask if I was okay."

"Look, I know you look wonderful and don't look like you've been kidnapped or on an uninhabited island with a maniac, but I didn't know. Then I finally got here, you have tons of other people here who also love you and care about you, and nobody bothered to tell me that you were even alive!

"Much to my surprise, the manager here at the resort, who I have threatened with every lawsuit I can think of, had no idea that

I still didn't know you were safe. He didn't contact me to let me know because he assumed you would have let me know."

"Yes, I'm fine," she whispered on the edge of tears as she thought, *"I feel like my heart is going to break."*

"Grace, you may not understand how difficult it has been for me, but I've constantly missed you. I've come to a shocking conclusion. I should have put a stop to this months ago."

Grace was trembling with anxiety as the sadness ran through her soul. *"Oh no! Joe, Please don't say it! Please! Don't end our friendship. I won't ever be able to stop loving you."*

As she lifted her eyes to meet his, a tear overflowed and ran down her cheek as her heart broke.

Joe had never seen her so moved, and it crossed his mind not to tell her how much he loved her. However, He heard his mother's voice, Saying, "Tell her you love her! We can't read your mind!"

He looked into Grace's eyes, saw that lone tear as his hand came up to move a lock of hair away from her eye, and softly said, "Grace, I can't help myself. I don't know how it happened, but I've fallen in love with you."

Grace tried to comprehend what he had just said. "Really? Is that what you needed to tell me?"

As Joe nodded yes, he took her in his arms, tilted her face to gaze into her eyes, and gave her a long, life-saving kiss. It was the sweetest thing he'd ever imagined.

After Grace caught her breath, she said, "Well, I'm not sure when it happened, but I've fallen in love with you too. I've spent the whole week wondering what it would be like if we kissed, but that kiss just went off the charts."

He didn't want to waste one more minute of their lives apart. They were in the middle of their second long kiss when Joe urgently needed to ask her an important question.

Joe gazed at Grace with love as he removed his grandmother's engagement ring from his pocket and knelt down on one knee.

He asked, "Grace Cook, would you please do me the honor of making me the happiest man on earth and agree to marry me?"

Grace cried, "Yes, I would love to marry you, Joe Lawrence!"

He slid the ring on her finger and took her in his arms again. He whispered in her ear, "I hope you're not going to want a long engagement because I want to start our life together as soon as possible."

Chapter 49

Later, Joe Lawrence spotted Grace's dad and started to wander in his direction by way of the refreshment table. Joe fixed him a small plate of finger food, including quiche, pineapple coconut coffee cake, and chocolate-covered strawberries. As Joe approached James Cook and handed him the plate and a cup of coffee, he said, "Here, James, I know this whole ordeal with Grace missing had to be hard on you. However, your connection involving Captain James Cook's locket and your family's key has got to be a huge deal!"

James thanked him and felt the hot liquid burning his throat as he sipped the coffee. "It's just hard to believe. I didn't even know why she was coming to Tahiti."

"We didn't even know she'd left the country until she called and said, 'Guess where I am? I'm in Tahiti!' She said she had something important to share with us, and we were supposed to join her here."

Joe explained, "Yes, I was in court all day, but I was supposed to call her at this resort in Tahiti. When I called her, she was already delayed returning from the flight in the yellow seaplane. It's unbelievable!"

They stood solemnly, trying to process the shock of it all.

A moment later, Joe said, "Oh, James, I need to talk with you!"

Joe raised his head and looked Grace's father in the eyes as he tried to explain, "I know this may seem like a wrong time to bring this up, but I've recently come to understand how important Grace is to me. I don't know how I missed it."

"I mean, I've realized that I've been falling in love with her for some time now. She's the first person I think of when I wake up. All my plans involve her. She's the last person I think of as I fall asleep at night.

"The thing I regret the most about this feeling is that I've never told her. I didn't recognize it myself. I guess you need to hit me over the head with this obvious news, but I was too busy setting up all my friends with the pranks and jokes about their love life that I missed the best part."

James felt his utter distress and quietly answered, "Well, Joe, this isn't news to me. I could see how you felt a mile away. You've always been good to Grace; her life has been more exciting and happy since you've been around each other."

"Wow," exclaimed Joe. "Well, I didn't know if Grace felt anything romantic toward me until we had the chance to talk about it."

Joe laughed as he continued, "I guess Grace already told you I asked her to marry me a little while ago. She even agreed and told me she loved me too."

James replied with a laugh also. "Congratulations to both of you. I think that's great!"

"Well," Joe admitted. "It really scares me that I may have messed up. Attorney Jeffery Williams from New York City flew halfway around the world to help her figure out this lighthouse cornerstone puzzle. I was praying that I wasn't too late."

Jim answered, "Well, Grace and this guy only share the historical side of each other. You have shared everything else with her, and that's been a valuable history on its own. You two know the enjoyment you share just being around each other. That stands the test of time. "

"Okay. Sir, that being said, I love your daughter! I mean the total, unconditional kind of love. I realize I've already asked Grace to marry me, and she's the most important thing in the world to me. I might have this backward, but it would mean a lot if we could have your blessing."

"Joe, I wouldn't give my blessing for Grace to marry anyone else but you!"

Chapter 50

Grace and her mom walked over to see what James and Joe were discussing.

Her dad hugged Grace and Sarah as he laughed joyfully and said, "Well, now I've gone and done it. I've just given these two my blessing to get married, Sarah."

Sarah gave her a tearful blessing too. "Now they are twice blessed! I'm so happy!"

Grace joined in, "Well, we are refusing to drag this engagement thing out. We've wasted enough time!"

That's when Maggie and Kate joined in the celebration.

"Oh My, look at that ring!" exclaimed Maggie. "That's stunning!"

Kate took Grace's hand and took a good look at the ring. Then she looked up at Joe and said, "Did you give this to Grace as an engagement ring?"

Joe answered, half humbly and half proudly, "Yes."

Kate looked at him in amazement and whispered, "Where did you get this, Joe? Did you come here with it in your pocket or something?"

Joe looked at Grace and kissed her softly. He lifted her hand to his lips. He looked into her eyes and lovingly said, "This was my grandmother's engagement ring. She wanted to remain in our family to be passed down through our lineage. It's been kept in my parent's safe deposit box at the bank."

Grace was shocked, "Joe, this is that ring? This is the ring we were talking about?" She laughed, "I can't believe it; we spent hours talking about the Victorian Era (1837-1901, which is the style of The Venus Pointe Lighthouse we saw today. It's wonderful! We need to go see it together! We covered all the periods and what happened during each period. The Victorian Era, Art Nouveau, and the Art Deco Era. We wondered if your grandmother's ring was styled in any particular design."

Joe agreed, "Yes, I couldn't remember exactly what it looked like or any details because I just saw it that day. However, I learned from the certificate my mom included with the ring that it was from the Late Edwardian / Early Art Deco era. I assume that would include the Art Nuevo period, which is between them."

He turned to the others and explained, "I had just passed the Bar Exam and was setting up my law practice in Sea Crest, and they were teasing me about all the money I was going to make. We were putting some things into the safe deposit box at the bank that day, and they showed me Grandma's ring. I didn't even have a girlfriend at the time, so it never came up again."

Maggie asked, "So, do your folks know you took it?"

"I didn't take it! My mom got it for me and sent it to me by courier when I gathered the documentation I needed for my passport. She knew I was in love with Grace, and I'd asked if I could use it for her engagement ring."

"Wait! I'm confused," cried Grace.

"Oh, I'm sorry, Grace. I'll get you a ring of your choice if you want."

"No, I love it! It means the world to me that you'd want to use it for our engagement. Thank you. Now, tell me about your passport!"

"Well, I never had one. I would have been here three days ago, but first, the TSA denied my boarding because of a mix-up with the tools in my duffle bag from my car. I scooped up the handles of it and carried it with my other carry-on bags. They made a terrible clink when I threw my stuff on the conveyer belt. Apparently, they don't allow sharp knives over 7" long and things that can be used as a weapon in carry-on baggage. By the time the TSA agents released me, I'd missed the last connecting flight to Tahiti."

"Wow! That's crazy."

"Yes, it was. Plus, I've constantly called the Tahiti Hilton Resort and your cell phone. I've threatened Mr. Allaire, the manager, with lawsuits for the resort, plus personal bodily harm if you were not safe and sound by the time I arrive here."

"Oh, dear!" Grace replied. "You wouldn't hurt a fly, Joe."

"Grace, you have no idea what I'd do if I lost you!" Joe said fiercely. "Why didn't you ever answer your phone?"

"My cell phone? I haven't had it for days. I was taking pictures with my phone when the seaplane flew into a flock of White Tern birds from the Tetiaroa Bird Sanctuary. We suffered a bird strike, and our engine was practically destroyed.

"My cell phone was smashed, and during the rain of bird body parts, I saw the last piece of my phone clutched in the claws of a dead bird as it dropped a hundred feet into the Pacific Ocean."

"Boy, I thought the worst when you never answered. It was awful," uttered Joe.

"Oh, I'm so sorry you worried about me," Grace said.

"Well, the further delay was caused when I tried to board my flight the following day. I was fine up to the point when they asked for my passport. Of course, I didn't have one. I've never gone anywhere that I needed one.

"That's when the airline ticket puncher told me about a new passport service that had opened up at the airport and could get me processed in about 24 hours. They use special couriers. I called Mom to get all the extra things I needed, and that's when I told her Grace was missing and possibly dead. I had realized that I truly love Grace, and she agreed that I should take Grandma's engagement ring to bring good luck and great happiness."

"She sent it with the courier, and I brought it to propose to the love of my life."

"By the way, we'd like to get married as soon as possible," Joe said in a dry, horse voice.

Maggie piped up with a perfect solution. "I'm sure I overheard our dear friend and ever-ready Chaplain O'Reilly offer to be available to help us in any way possible. I believe there is a 45-day waiting period for the paperwork to be completed in Tahiti."

Kate stated, "However, there is no waiting time if you're married by Chaplain O'Reilly on the United States Coast Guard Cutter. We could fly you out. That would give you a legal marriage good in the United States and elsewhere."

Joe said, "Then we could fly back, and the Chaplain would finish your ceremony ...

Everyone joined in to finish;... "At the top of the Venus Pointe Lighthouse!"

"What a wonderful idea!" Grace declared. "Let's do it tomorrow!"

A universal cheer went up, including everyone from the guests – to the hotel staff!

Chapter 51

The following morning Grace and her entourage of fashion experts entered the upscale women's boutique in the Tahiti Hilton Resort. Her friends and mom were determined to find their newest bride a spectacular wedding gown for her wedding.

Luckily, due to her food consumption (or lack thereof), during her recent vacation on an uninhabited island for several days, Grace was at the best weight she'd been since high school.

Mind you, that's not to say she didn't have a plentiful supply of coconuts, pineapples, and hand-caught fish. She also sported the very best tan of her entire life. Man, she looked great!

Sarah Cook reminded her daughter, "Grace, are you really going to get married today?"

"Yes, Mom. That's exactly what we're going to do."

Her mother smiled and advised, "Well, you're going to have to find a gown or dress off the rack. There will be no time for alterations."

"I already thought all about that. I should be able to find a perfect wedding dress, even if we need to steal it off the mannequin. In fact, one of us should be in charge of checking out the window displays in these wedding boutiques."

Mary Beth volunteered. "I'd be great at that. I also think they put the smallest sizes on the mannequins. With your new skinny look, that should fit fine. Do you think your shoe size decreased too?"

"Hey, Hey, Hey," laughed Grace. "I have been thinking I need something with a removable train or no train, so I don't have to walk up to the top of the lighthouse with it tripping me. I know I want my extra sun-drenched blonde long hair swept back and held with a small flower piece of white roses."

Kate joked, "Isn't it amazing what a few days stranded on an uninhabited island can do for your classic bridal beauty. It looks like you've spent those days at a beauty spa!"

"I know what you mean. When I returned and looked in the mirror, I had to look twice to be sure it was me."

Grace caught a glimpse of the bridal shop window, and they all came to a screeching stop!

There in the window was a long white gown. It had a Trumpet/Mermaid Tulle Applique V-neck Sleeveless/ Brush train Wedding Dress. It was a show-stopper, for sure! The mannequin had long sun-bleached hair, swept back in a wave, with loose soft curls around her face. It had a floral comb made of several white roses. It was shocking to see how beautiful it was.

"Wow," whispered Grace, "This window display is simple but so classic that it's absolutely stunning."

"Let's go in," said Mary Beth. "I think that dress would fit you perfectly!"

They all filed into the shop on a mission.

The shop owner was smiling as she greeted them, "Hello. Welcome to my shop. I see you're interested in my latest design."

"Yes, we love that gown in the window. Can I try it on?" beamed Grace.

"As a matter of fact, I just finished it last night. I was having a cup of tea and praying for that poor girl that was lost at sea. Our whole town is so brokenhearted over that tragedy. And Philip was such a nice boy. Well, as I finished up and was drying my cup and saucer, the phone rang. It was my friend who works at the Tahiti Hilton Resort with the news."

With tears overflowing her eyes, she imparted the joyful tidings, "The girl was saved! Can you believe it? The phone lines for the whole island were so overloaded last night that we almost lost power. It's a miracle!"

"I suddenly felt inspired to finish the dress. It's the most special dress I've designed. It was made with feelings of hope, and I prayed with great faith for these young people. This is what this dress represents."

During her whole emotional explanation, no one said a word.

She hurried over to the window and proceeded to take it down. She turned to Grace with a gentle smile and said, "something just told me to finish it and make sure I had it in the front window when I opened this morning. It looks like it may be a perfect fit."

Grace took a step toward the lady with open arms and hugged her as she said, "Thanks for your prayers! I'm that blessed girl you were praying for, and I'm so grateful."

"This is my mother, Sarah Cook, who flew here, and all my friends came to help find me."

Of course, there were tears all around with hugs.

The dress fit like a glove and looked spectacular.

Chapter 52

Maggie, Kate, and Joe quickly called the Coast Guard Cutter in the area.

Kate asked to speak with Chaplain O'Reilly. They got him on the line, and Kate said, "Hello, Chaplain. This is Coast Guard Search and Rescue Pilot Kate Jensen.

"Well, hello. How are things going with Grace? It was a pleasure to meet her yesterday. I've got you here with Maggie Jensen and Grace's good friend, Attorney Joseph Lawrence."

"Great, I know I've met you at the celebration Joseph."

"Hello, and you may call me Joe."

"Okay, what can I do for you folks?"

"Well, Joe and Grace are engaged to be married, and they'd love to do it as soon as possible.

"Wow!" he laughed. "Well, if you're asking me to officiate, I'll make myself available. You just say the word."

"Thank you, Chaplain, but there's a catch."

"I'm listening."

Kate explained, "We understand that Tahiti has a 45-day waiting period to process the paperwork if you're an international couple. Then they call the couple and tell them their date."

"Their first choice was to be married at the top of the Venus Pointe Lighthouse today, but of course, that will not work," said Maggie.

"How can I help?" asked the Chaplain.

Maggie continued, "Kate and I thought maybe you'd agree to legally marry them on the Coast Guard Cutter today. Then accompany them to the top of the Venus Pointe Lighthouse and remarry them again in a ceremony where they will 'renew their vows,' which is allowed."

Joe said, "Chaplain Grace has just verified that her father is a descendant of the Captain James Cook family. That means Grace will be the first ancestor of the Cook family to marry at the Venus Pointe Lighthouse. That is not only a historical milestone, but an epic celebration!"

Chaplain O'Reilly declared, "I will be honored to be part of this amazing double-wedding event. Do you know what time you'd like the Cutter wedding and what time you'd like the lighthouse wedding?

Maggie said, "Grace has her wedding gown, and her hair should be done by now."

The Chaplain asked, "Who will attend the first wedding ceremony?"

"Here's the wish list. Grace's parents, James and Sarah Cook, The bride's three attendants, Maggie, Mary Beth and Kate, and Joe, who do you want for your Best Man? Jeffrey Williams and Mr. Allaire?"

Joe said, "Grace and I called my folks yesterday after we were engaged. They called me an hour later and said they were on a connecting flight to Tahiti. They arrive here within the hour."

The Chaplain suggested, "Why don't we shuttle everyone over to the Coast Guard Cutter. That's only about ten family and friends. Why don't they surround the couple in a circle when the ceremony starts? It gives the wedding an intimate, loving feeling."

"Yes, that's perfect," said Joe.

"That ceremony will be fairly short, but I'll certainly make it meaningful," promised the Chaplain.

Joe's cell phone rang, and the text showed that his parents had just arrived. He said, "I'm going to meet my folks at the lobby. I'll check them in and let them know that Grace and I are getting married shortly. Maggy, would you please see if Grace is ready and tell her I'll meet her at the Coast Guard Cutter and bring her passport for ID for the marriage license? Thank you."

Chapter 53

Joe greeted and hugged his mom and dad in the lobby. "Hello, I'm so glad you could make it!"

"We're so happy that you've asked Grace to marry you. I'm sure your engagement will be a wonderful time for you, leading up to your marriage," said his dad.

"Yes, It's been great! Now we're on our way out to that Coast Guard Cutter to get married," he announced happily.

"When?" asked his mom.

"Right now, as a matter of fact! We didn't want a long engagement, so we're taking advantage of our family and friends here on Tahiti."

"You're kidding!" exclaimed his mom. "Well, I, for one, am thrilled to death."

"It's come as you are. Casual is fine. I understand Grace went out and got a wedding dress this morning. Since we're not supposed to see each other on our wedding day, I'm not sure how it's all going. But I love Grace to the ends of the earth!"

"Let's take your bags to your room, and we can freshen up if you'd like. Then it's off to the ship. The Coast Guard Chaplain is going to officiate at the wedding."

"After the legal ceremony, we're going to come back to the Venus Pointe Lighthouse and have an additional ceremony at the top of the lighthouse. Grace will be Captain James Cook's family's only ancestor to be married at the lighthouse."

Joe's father asked, "So this means you'll get married twice today?"

"Yes, since we aren't a Tahitian or French Polynesian, we'd have to wait for 45-days for them to clear the paperwork and give us a wedding date. However, we still want to have a wedding here. Their government will allow us to renew our wedding vows, so we'll have two ceremonies today."

Kate flew a helicopter back and forth over the next half-hour, so everyone could gather at the chapel in the Coast Guard Cutter.

Two Coast Guard musicians started to play Passacaglia, the poignant duet on the violin and the viola.

Grace walked into the chapel in her beautiful white wedding gown, designed and sewn with faith and blessings woven into the hope for Grace's rescue.

Grace's hair had turned out exactly as she'd planned. It was drawn up on the sides, with a small whispy ponytail over the loosely curled, long hair cascading part-way down her back. She had a beautiful design of white roses on the back of her hair. Her sun-drenched hair was doubly blond, set off by her deep tan. She was carrying a bouquet of white roses.

Joe thought, *"Wow, I've never seen anyone so beautiful. The dress looks like it was made especially for Grace."*

Grace handed the white roses to Mary Beth. Joe reached out for Grace's hand, and she stepped to stand beside him, as the ceremony began and the marriage vows were spoken.

Chaplin O'Reilly read a Biblical passage from 1 Corinthians 13, which explained Love and ended with, '*And now Abide faith, hope, love, these three; but the greatest of these is love.*'

"I now pronounce you husband and wife! You may now kiss the bride!"

Chapter 54

Once they returned to The Tahiti Hilton Resort, the Manager invited them to have a reception. "We are honored to welcome the happy couple and guests to our special Steak and Lobster Restaurant.

His following statement was primarily due to his relief that He and The Tahiti Hilton Resort were not getting sued. *"By the time Joe set foot in the hotel, Grace was here 'Safe and Sound!' I'm still unsure what happened to Philip, but I was told that was privileged international information. I was to ask no questions and say nothing!"*

He announced proudly, "Of course, there will be no charge to any and all of the guests. We are happy to be of service."

The manager asked to speak to Joe and Grace privately at the check-in counter. As they followed him over, He talked about how beautiful Grace looked.

"Thank you!" Grace answered. "I was so pleased to be able to buy this precious gown from the window of the first shop I stopped at this morning."

Joe admired her as he softly said, "I don't think I've ever seen a dress this beautiful in my life. Where did you say it came from?"

"I'm so blessed, Joe. I went out this morning with my mom, Mary Beth, Maggie, and Kate. We were hoping against hope that we'd be able to find something suitable for me to wear today. After all, I came to Tahiti to see if I was a relative of Captain James Cook and researched the Venus Pointe Lighthouse. I wasn't planning to wear a dress the whole time. I didn't bring one. So anyway, we went out to see if we could find anything 'off the rack' that would be nice enough for me to wear. Well, our first shop had this stunning gown in the window.

"The owner was the designer and the seamstress of the gown. She said she'd been praying for that girl who was lost at sea. Last night, her friend called and relayed that the girl had been found. The friend was an employee here at the resort. She'd said the girl was safe and sound. The shop owner was so inspired that she worked into the night to complete this dress.

"This morning, she had just dressed the manikin and placed it in the window when we walked in. It's a real miracle, but it fits me perfectly. I thanked her for praying for me and told her I was the missing girl."

"Wow, if that's not a miracle, I don't know what is," replied Joe.

The manager said, "That's not the end of the miracle. When the employee told me about her designer friend, it reminded me of a long-lost love of mine. We met at the university in Paris. She was always drawing and sewing the most beautiful creations. We went to one of the bridges in Paris and put our love lock on the bridge. When her family discovered we were in love, they forbade her to continue seeing me."

"We were young, but we were deeply in love. We planned to secretly get married, but her folks pulled her out of university, and I never knew where she was or what happened to her.

"My employee told me about the seamstress, and I went to see her today while you were getting married. She opened the door of her shop, and we both almost fainted. I was a little more prepared than she was, but she's still the one I dream about. Neither of us ever married.

"She was designing her beautiful creations just steps away from me, and our paths never crossed. We are getting married next Saturday."

Chapter 55

The manager told them, "I also have a nice surprise for you newlyweds. We'd like to move both of your belongings to the "Honeymoon Suite," but we need your permission."

Joe and Grace both laughed, "Yes! That would be great! Thank you!"

Grace asked, "By the way, do you know anything about those over-the-water bungalows on Bora, Bora?"

"Yes, as a matter of fact, I got transferred from there about 3 months ago. The Hilton Nui Bora Bora. They even have two luxury, over-the-water bungalows that have two stories. They are villas (1001 & 1002). They offer 2 bedrooms, 2 dressing rooms, 3 bathrooms, and a private sun deck on the lower level. The upper floor has a well-being room with facilities for massage and sauna, plus a large outdoor living area with a jacuzzi, sundeck, bar area, deck chairs, and dining table. Would you like me to set up a transfer for you for tomorrow?"

Joe smiled, "That sounds great. Do you have a brochure, Grace? Let's see our families' plans before deciding which day to transfer."

"Here are some other things that might interest you, said the manager. "I usually advise people to get brand new snorkeling masks and fins. They typically bring theirs from home. They are much more sanitary, and you don't have to wait for rentals or sizes to be available.

"It won't help you for this trip, but did you know you can have the glass in your mask made for your eyeglass prescription. I don't know about bi-focal masks, but they would improve your visibility if you need to see them more precisely."

Joe said, "Wow, I'll keep that in mind for the future; however, I'll tell my folks about it today. Thanks!"

"Great," continued the Manager. "One of my favorite things in the over-the-water bungalows is the coffee table with a removable clear glass top. You can see beautiful fish underwater. It's like a glass-bottom boat. Then if you want to swim and snorkel around your bungalow, you can.

"You can also feed the fish in the water when you remove the glass top of the coffee table. The resort will supply you with food every day to feed them.

"It's also fun to take a catamaran ride. The islands are beautiful, and we have a unique opportunity to admire spinner dolphins, pilot whales, and pelagic sharks. Every year between July and early November, humpback whales migrate through the warm Polynesian waters.

"You can even swim with humpback whales."

Chapter 56

The Tahiti Hilton had the atrium set up for refreshments. The manager handed the chaplain a battery-operated CD player and explained, "This is beautiful music we use for some of our weddings. You're welcome to use it while your guests climb up to the top of the lighthouse. And before the wedding, (rehearsal) ceremony starts. I also have a small microphone for you to use. Sometimes the crashing waves make it hard to hear. It will also help if any of your guests are afraid of heights or have trouble climbing so many stairs. They might stay below in the park and sit on the benches. It's delightful."

The limo drivers transported the wedding party and guests to the lighthouse when they were ready to depart. Joe told the Chaplain, "Grace and I have a few words to say to each other. I guess you could call them our vows."

"Yes, that would be great, he said."

Well, the wedding was on the move as the guests loaded into the limos and headed for the following location. They were delighted by the beautiful scenery as they approached the Venus Pointe Lighthouse.

Some of the guests chose to observe from the ground as Joe and Grace, their parents, and Chaplain O'Reilly climbed the steps of The Venus Pointe Lighthouse to renew their vows. Grace's father and mother were especially eager to climb the steps of the structure built to honor their ancestor. Joe's parents also wanted to join them at the top, and his mom had brought something special to include in the ceremony.

The chaplain handed the CD Player to Kate and Maggie. They saw the recordings on the disk and happily agreed to take care of the wedding's music. The music started as the wedding party ascended to the top level and stepped out to the balcony surrounding the lantern room, called the galleries. The first piece was a piano selection called 'Celebrated Kanon' by Dan Troxell. The notes filled the air as the music streamed flawlessly from the player. The renewal ceremony was briefly delayed while they caught their breath at the top.

When Grace and Joe approached the railing, they were greeted by a few of their family and friends below. They looked far out to sea and enjoyed the immense beauty of the blue and green waves as they crashed into the beach below.

The Chaplain started the ceremony, "I'd like to welcome everyone to the second wedding event of the day for Joe and Grace Lawrence!"

Everyone laughed and cheered!

The Chaplain continued, "The bride and groom will exchange Flower Leis. In French Polynesia, a Lei is given on every joyous occasion. Indeed, in the celebration of a wedding, the Lei represents the Joy of Life. Like a wedding ring, the Lei is also an unbroken circle representing your eternal commitment and devotion to each other."

Each wore a lei of white flowers around their neck for this ceremony. They exchanged them to signify their pledge to help and love each other.

The Chaplain said, "I understand you have written some vows. Please share them at this time."

Grace and Joe had some kind words to recite, and it was truly touching to hear them speak from the heart about feelings they had never spoken out loud about before.

Joe looked into Grace's eyes and said,

"Grace, The time I spend with you fills me with joy,

I promise to love and cherish you, now and forever!

You mean the world to me!

Thank you for sharing your life with me."

Grace had tears in her eyes as she said,

"Joe. You're the kindest, funniest, most enjoyable man I've ever met.

I love you with all my heart!

You're the first thing I think about when I wake up and,

the last thing I think about as I fall asleep.

I'd be lost without you!

Thank you for sharing your life with me!"

As they kissed, they felt a deep love that their wedding vows had represented.

Chaplain O'Reilly was pleasantly surprised at a depth of their feelings. He thought, "Maybe I should say some of those things to my wife. They seem to have a deep appreciation of the value of human life. Wow, of course, they do. Grace has been lost at sea and on an uninhabited island for days. Joe was worried that he'd never see her again. Yes, that can give you a sense of wisdom that normally comes with old age."

The Chaplain stated, "It's just a formality, but I'll ask anyway. Would you like to exchange rings?"

"Both fathers looked at each other smiling as they answered, "Yes!"

Grace and Joe looked surprised as Joe's mother handed him a ring and said, "This is your grandmother's wedding ring that pairs with her engagement ring. We'd like you to have it."

Joe accepted the ring and kissed his mother. "This is stunning! Thank you!"

Grace's mother handed her a ring also. "We went to the resort gift shop with Joe's parents today, after your first wedding. We picked out a wedding band for Joe that matches the wedding ring that Joe's grandmother had."

The parents said, "You can change them out later if you'd like something else."

"No, this is perfect!" said Grace as she hugged and kissed her mother.

They each slipped the wedding rings on the ring fingers of each other's hands.

The chaplain blessed their marriage and said, "I now pronounce you husband and wife again. You may now kiss your bride!" There was sheer happiness at the Venus Pointe Lighthouse.

The music for, *The River is Wide,* filled the air as they descended from the glorious ceremony. This double wedding would be remembered forever by everyone who attended.

Keep Reading for an excerpt from

The Masquerade Ball at the Lighthouse

The fourth book in

The Sea Crest Lighthouse Series.

By Carolyn Court

~♥~

Mary Beth froze to stare at the masked figure who had just arrived at the Sea Crest Lighthouse Masquerade Ball! Her dance partner awkwardly stumbled and stepped on her foot. *"What's happening?"* Jeffrey Williams wondered. "Excused me," he muttered in surprise. However, she never heard him.

Mary Beth removed her hand from Jeffrey's and covered her mouth in shock! She didn't comprehend a single thing that he'd said as she thought, *"I have literally dreamed of this man for years! Granted, he is masked, but so is the man of my dreams. The star of the two 'Zorro' movies!"*

"Who is he? And where on earth did this guy come from?"

The undercover DEA agent with the newly created identity took this all in with utter delight. Antonio slowly approached the band leader. As he passed his request note with a substantial tip to the man, he said, *'s'il vous plaît?'* (If you Please?)

The band leader read the note, smiled, and said, *'c'est mon plaisir!'* (It's my pleasure!)

As the band began playing the theme music from *The Mask of Zorro,* Antonio turned and looked for Mary Beth. He smiled when he saw her dazzling silver Flapper costume. *"Wow, Now that's indescribably awesome! This is going to be fun!"* He walked straight toward her, never taking his eyes off her.

Mary Beth thought, *"Wow, I must be dreaming."*

However, Jeffrey wasn't feeling so dreamy as he watched this strange attraction play out. He wondered, *"Who is this guy? I'm going to have Maggie run a check on him as soon as possible!"*

By this time, Antonio was right in front of her. He held out his hand as he thought, *"Wow, what a knockout!"*

What he actually whispered was, *"Puis-je avoir cette danse?"* (May I have this dance?)

All Mary Beth could utter was, "Oui," As she took his hand. ("Yes,")

He took her in his arms, and they danced away.

On the other hand, Jeffrey Williams was left standing, wondering, *"What just happened? The nerve of that guy! He didn't even say, May I cut in! It was like Mary Beth was in a trance or something!"*

Meanwhile, the rude intruder reflected on how wonderful Mary Beth felt in his arms. *"Wow, Grace told me that Mary Beth had a crush on Antonio Banderas, but she didn't ever mention how beautiful she was. She is so graceful; she could be a professional dancer. I love dancing with her. I also loved spotting her from across the room in the silver Flapper dress Grace told me she'd be wearing."*

Meanwhile, Grace and Joe enjoyed observing how their latest setup was going. They're up to their old tricks again. When asked what kind of wedding celebration they wanted when the newlyweds returned to Sea Crest, they both agreed they'd like a Masquerade Ball at the lighthouse. "We'll hire the same company that provided the wonderful dance space for Kate and Michael's wedding celebration. We want the same design they had on the beach beneath the Sea Crest Lighthouse. Those click-together blocks that lit up were marvelous."

Grace and Joe secretly devised their usually clandestine pranks to throw these two together.

Maggie watched her old partner closely. He seemed much quieter than usual. "Hey, I saw you last night dancing with Mary Beth; then you were gone. What happened? Did she step on your foot or something?"

"Goodness, no! She's a great dancer. Is she a professional?"

"No, but she loves music, and she's taken dance lessons her entire life. I'm pretty sure she occasionally teaches as a substitute at the Sea Crest Dance Studio. Then, of course, she teaches some special dance classes annually."

"Like what? The tango?" laughed Antonio.

"As a matter of fact, that's one of her favorites! She loves to tango! That's why she started up those classes. She needed somebody to tango with!"

"You're kidding, right?"

"No, I'm serious! Now lots of us know how to tango. If you'd stuck around last night, you'd have seen lots of us dancing. Of course, we're not as good as Mary Beth, but we're good enough to enjoy ourselves."

"By the way, what did happen to you last night? You suddenly disappeared," she said.

When he didn't answer immediately, Maggie prodded him, "I hope she didn't say anything to upset you. That's hardly like her."

"No, of course, she didn't say anything offensive. As a matter of fact, she didn't say anything except "Oui" when I asked her to dance," he said under his breath.

"Wow, she answered in French? How strange."

"Yes," answered Antonio. "I'd asked her in French, and that's how she answered. It just rolled off her tongue like it was the most natural thing in the world. Then we started to dance and believe me, I danced with the best of them. It's just never felt so unexpectedly perfect. I'm trying to figure out if it's because I was so surprised by how beautiful she looked."

"Well, did you think she'd be some kind of a troll or something?"

"I knew she'd had a crush on Zorro, and I guess if I knew what she was like, looks, grace, speaks French flawlessly, etc., I wouldn't have been so eager to play a prank on her. I felt terrible."

"Well," said Maggie. "What happened to you?"

"When we danced by the potted trees by the edge of the dance floor, I spun her around, into a 1½ turn spin and I stepped off the floor, behind the plants, and kept going. I never looked back."

~♥~

Characters: The Cornerstone of the Lighthouse, The Sea Crest Lighthouse Series, Book 3

Grace Cook – Protagonist   Sea Crest Historian – 3rd Mah Jongg Player

Joe Lawrence – Best friend and love interest - Best Attorney in Sea Crest

Philip – Tahiti Hilton Resort handyman - Flies and Tinkers with his Little Yellow Seaplane

Mr. Allaire - Tahiti Hilton Resort Manager

Mary Beth, one of Grace's friends & 4th Mah Jongg player – wants to return to France

Grace's parents, James and Sara Cook

Kate Jensen – Married to Michael Jensen - Book One - U.S. Coast Guard Search and Rescue Pilot 1st Mah Jongg Player

Michael Jensen – Renowned Lighthouse Architect – Repairing Sea Crest Lighthouse

Maggie Jensen - Married to James Jensen – Book Two – FBI Special Agent - 2nd Mah Jongg Player

James Jensen – NYC Finacial Advisor –

Attorney Jeffrey Williams - Chambers' New York City Lawyer - Board member of the Captain James Cook Society in New York City.

Pierre - Tahiti Historian

Jacque – Tahiti limo driver

Mr. Teva– Manager of the Venus Pointe Lighthouse, Tahiti

Ms. Alana Flores, Tahiti Museum curator -

Mr. and Mrs. Lawrence   - Joe's Parents

Recipes

For special dishes and desserts from

The Key to the Lighthouse Cornerstone

<u>Sweet Crepes</u>

1 ¼ cups flour

dash of salt

¼ cup of sugar

1 egg

1 ¼ cups of milk

2 Tablespoons butter melted

Vegetable oil or butter for greasing pan

Mix flour, salt, sugar, egg, milk, and melted butter together.

Heat a non-stick pan or skillet.

Grease pan with butter or oil.

Pour batter into a hot pan.

<u>Pineapple and Walnut Crepes</u>

Add crushed pineapple and chopped walnuts for filling

Chocolate Mousse

4 large egg yolks

4 tablespoons sugar

2 cups heavy cream

8 squares – 1 oz each of bittersweet chocolate, melted

1 teaspoon vanilla extract

Melt the chocolate in a double boiler or a metal heat-proof bowl placed over a saucepan of boiling water. Stir as chocolate is melting. Remove from heat when melted to cool slightly.

Butter Dishes & Set aside.

In the bowl of a stand mixer (a hand mixer may also be used), beat egg whites on high until frothy; add the lemon juice.

Continue to beat egg whites, slowly adding the granulated sugar a few tablespoons at a time (allow to mix in before adding more). Beat eggs until stiff but not dry.

Stir egg yolks into the chocolate. Gently stir a third of the egg white mixture into the chocolate.

Combine the chocolate mixture into the bowl with the egg white mixture and gently mix together.

Spoon the mousse mixture into the prepared dishes.

Cover and thoroughly chill before serving.

Pineapple Angel Food Cake

Dottie Lohr

1 Box of angel food cake mix

15 oz can crushed pineapple (undrained)

Use any brand of cake mix.

Follow the directions on the box.

Add pineapple.

Bake and enjoy!

Crunch Topped Oriental Chicken

Carolyn Durphy

Preheat the oven to 375 degrees

4 to 6 servings

1 – 1lb-4-1/2oz can pineapple chunks in heavy syrup

¼ cup butter

¼ cup chopped green pepper

¼ cup chopped onion

¼ cup sliced celery

¼ cup firmly packed light brown sugar

2-1/2 T cornstarch

½ t salt

2 T soy sauce

¼ t Worchestershire sauce

2 cups water, including pineapple liquid

2 to 3 lbs cut-up skinless chicken

Cooked rice for 4 to 6 people

In a 2-quart saucepan, melt butter and add green pepper, celery, and onion, and sauté for 3 minutes.

Stir in brown sugar, cornstarch, and salt.

Remove from heat and stir in soy sauce, Worcestershire sauce, and reserved liquid.

Cook over medium heat, constantly stirring, until thickened.

Remove from heat and add pineapple.

Place chicken in a 13x9 baking pan and pour sauce over all.

Bake for an hour and 15 minutes or until tender.

Remove from the oven and place on a platter over the hot cooked rice.

Top with crushed potato chips

Gary & Wendy's Pizza

Gary and Wendy Courtright

1 Cup of Bread Flour

1 pkg. instant raid Dry Yeast

1 Cup hot water

Blend Flour & Yeast

Gradually stir in hot water

Add flour until proper consistency

Gather into a log/roll

If more than 1 recipe, cut unto sections.

Roll into balls, flour, and put in floured bowl to rise

Roll out and spread in pizza pan

Make topping of our choice:

Pepperoni, sausage, tomatoes, peppers, etc.

Top with grated mozzarella cheese

Stuffed Eggplant

Louise Fletcher

1 Eggplant cut lengthwise in half

Scrap or carve out the insides. Set aside

Leave 2" of the outside shell

Chop Ground Pork (or Beef) with sauce, Regu, or other

1T. Garlic

Pinch pepper

Dash of salt

1T Rosemary

1T Oregano

1T olive oil   Mix into sauce

Mix well and pat into eggplant shell

Bake at 325°

<u>Chicken Parmesan</u>

Louise Fletcher

Bake 6-8 Chicken thighs

Make tomato sauce or use Regu or other favorite sauce

1T. Garlic

1T. Oregano

2 Teaspoons of Olive oil

½ cup of chopped celery

½ cup of Grated Cheese: Parmesan cheese

Mix well with chicken

Cook on the stove for about 1 hour

Serve with Pasta, Ziti, or your favorite

Acknowledgments

Special thanks to my brother Gary and his wonderful wife Wendy for their family recipe for pizza. I've heard that you two made 19 pizzas one time for your huge extended family. Everyone who's had the pleasure of eating your pizzas loves them.

Carolyn Durphy. Thanks for sharing your Crunch Topped Oriental Chicken recipe. I'm sure it's one of your family's favorites. I've always enjoyed your positive outlook on life and your wonderful sense of humor.

Louis Fletcher, you are famous for your distinguished acting career, which brings us all joy, laughter, and sometimes tears. However, your famous Italian Cooking is outstanding! Thanks for explaining how you make your delicious Chicken Parmesan and Stuffed Eggplant. We love Italian food, and we love you! You deserve a Standing Ovation!

Dottie Lohr. Thanks for the moist and yummy Pineapple Angel Food Cake recipe. You are one of my most supportive friends. As soon as I asked you about a recipe, you spouted this cake recipe just off the top of your head. You've been a positive contact, always looking for anything that might help my lighthouse-themed writing. I appreciate your kindness.

Jeanette Embrey, thanks for letting your pug, Snarfy, bless the pages of book 3, *The Key to the Lighthouse Cornerstone.* He's a riot to be around, and if he could read, I think he'd like Chapter 10 the best.

Thanks for your support with the numerous projects I have dreamed up. You are a wonderful friend and a fierce Mah Jongg competitor.

Thanks to the fantastic women in my weekly Mah Jongg groups who are great at outsmarting each other. These include, in no particular order, Sandy, Linda, Mary, Jeanette, Sheila, and Sandra.

My husband, Paul. Thanks for supporting me in my writing. You thought I had some interesting stories to tell. You even gave me my favorite Swiss Army knife, the Victorinox, for Christmas, years before I went to Tahiti. You're the best!

Marie and Mike Reeves. Thanks for introducing me to your delightful pug, Louie. He patrols the neighborhood and strives to keep us all safe. He's sure to leave his pawprint on the hearts of all who meet him. Thanks for letting him attend the dog park and have play dates on the pages of my book.

Information found in this book:

https://en.wikipedia.org/wiki/Giardia_lamblia

Tahiti Information:

https://en.wikivoyage.org/wiki/Tahiti

https://en.wikipedia.org/wiki/Historian

Amelia Earhart Information:

https://roadtoamelia.org/

https://sciencetrends.com/it-appears-amelia-earharts-body-has-finally-been-found/

https://www.prnewswire.com/news-releases/earharts-elusive-electra-is-the-hunt-over-301454872.html

https://www.nationalgeographic.com/adventure/article/amelia-earhart-search-island-dogs

Donovan Hohn Author of Moby-Duck

https://www.amazon.com/Moby-duck-True-Story-Bath-Toys/dp/1908526025

Captain James Cook

https://www.bing.com/search?q=was+Cap%27t+James+Cook+a+Freemason%3F&form=ANNTH1&refig=3

https://en.wikipedia.org/wiki/Historian

https://en.wikipedia.org/wiki/Point_Venus

http://nealslighthouses.blogspot.com/2009/02/pointe-venus.html

https://natlib.govt.nz/records/37988463

Survival

https://adventure.howstuffworks.com/survival/gear/top-5-survival-signals.htm

https://www.webmd.com/women/features/travelers-advisory

Shelter on an uninhabited Island:

Acidophilus pills for travel -

Travel Abroad Supplement | 60 Capsules - Optibac Probioticshttps://www.optibacprobiotics.com/product/probioti

https://adventure.howstuffworks.com/survival/gear/top-5-survival-signals.htm

https://www.alamy.com/stock-photo-bamboo-trees-in-a-forest-papeete-tahiti-french-polynesia-49911209.html

https://www.youtube.com/watch%3Fv%3DtCCdSrtK8OU

http://www.jewelsonninth.ca/jewels-blog/2016/9/30/mac-is-backand-hes-brought-his-trusty-swiss-army-knife-with-

him#:~:text=1985%2D1992%20MacGyver's%20most%20used,out%20of%20a%20tricky%20situation

Survival on a deserted island

https://www.youtube.com/watch%3Fv%3DtCCdSrtK8OU

https://www.wbur.org/npr/134923863/moby-duck-when-28-800-bath-toys-are-lost-at-sea

Info on Pugs:

https://dogtime.com/dog-breeds/pug#

http://www.pugs.co.uk/about-pugs/history/

Tahiti general info

https://www.youtube.com/watch%3Fv%3DtCCdSrtK8OU

https://www.firstclasswatches.co.uk/blog/2021/06/10-interesting-facts-about-aquamarine/

https://specialtyproduce.com/produce/Queen_Tahiti_Pineapples_15916.php

https://www.alamy.com/pineapple-plant-growing-in-the-wild-on-a-french-polynesia-island-image311424956.html (picture)

https://en.wikipedia.org/wiki/Native_American_the_great_dying

https://www.instagram.com/p/Bg7XCAIHnXk

https://today.uconn.edu/2011/05/ever-the-twain-shall-meet/#

https://localwiki.org/hsl/Mark_Twain

https://www.viator.com/tours/Moorea/Swim-with-humpback-whales

About the author (Carolyn Zacheis)

Pen Name: Carolyn Court

Carolyn Court is a writer of romantic suspense novels. She's a member of The United States Lighthouse Society and The Chesapeake Lights Chapter. She has visited lighthouses in Asia, Europe, the Caribbean, the USA, the Galapagos Islands, and Tahiti. She was a longtime member of the Caribbeans Tourist Board in Washington, D.C. She weaves historical events and known people into her storylines. She references her research so readers can follow up on areas of particular interest. The Venus Pointe Lighthouse in Tahiti is actual. This book is based on her visit to that lighthouse and her trip to several French Polynesian islands, including Tahiti and Bora, Bora.

Made in the USA
Middletown, DE
26 October 2022

13554858R00135